The Road to Jewel Beach

The Road to Jewel Beach

Christopher Adamson

June 7, 2017

For cousin Michael,

Genealogist Extraordinaire

& so much more!

Christopher

TORONTO

Exile Editions

2004

This edition is published by Exile Editions Limited, 20 Dale Avenue, Toronto, Ontario, Canada   M4W 1K4

Sales Distribution:
McArthur & Company   c/o Harper Collins
1995 Markham Road, Toronto, ON M1B 5M8
toll free: 1 800 387 0117   (fax) 1 800 668 5788

Composition and Design by MICHAEL CALLAGHAN
Cover Painting by GABRIELA CAMPOS
Typeset at MOONS OF JUPITER, TORONTO, ONTARIO
Printed and Bound at GAUVIN IMPRIMERIE, HULL, QUEBEC

Use of lyrics from the song "Wolverton Mountain," written by Merle Kilgore, is gratefully acknowledged.

This is a work of fiction. Names, characters, places, and incidents either are the product of the author's imagination or are used fictitiously, and any resemblance to actual persons, living or dead, events, or locales is entirely coincidental.

The Canada Council | Le Conseil des Arts
FOR THE ARTS | DU CANADA
SINCE 1957 | DEPUIS 1957

ONTARIO ARTS COUNCIL
CONSEIL DES ARTS DE L'ONTARIO

The publisher wishes to acknowledge the assistance toward publication of the Canada Council and the Ontario Arts Council.

ISBN 1-55096-617-0

for

W & M

Contents

VANCOUVER / 1

SEATTLE / 13

THE ROOF / 26

THE ROAD / 40

MULTNOMAH COUNTY HOSPITAL / 52

THE SIXTH FLOOR / 66

JEWEL BEACH / 75

VANCOUVER

Martha Spencer's bedroom fronted onto Denman Street but didn't get any natural light because Terry had painted in the windows. So people in the office building across the street couldn't see in. The only problem with the apartment was Nick's Grill. A constant odor of bacon grease and fish batter wafted up from below, and it couldn't be masked by the burning of incense or by the liberal spraying of scented air fresheners.

It was early afternoon when Martha got up off the mattress on the floor, stretched, then tiptoed into the kitchen, her feet pale against the scuffed pink linoleum. Ordinarily, you could hear voices in the whir of the ventilator out back, but Sundays were quiet. She cleared two un-eaten slices of pizza from the counter, then poured herself a glass of Chablis and curled up on the sagging maroon sofa in the living room, a room stuffed with wounded furniture, creaky high-back chairs that needed reupholstering, scratched pewter end tables, and antique lamps with frayed, dangerous-looking cords. She flipped through the books piled on the coffee table — *Moroccan Cuisine, Edith Partridge's Herb Cookbook, Chocolate Decadence*. Terry was forever hunting down new recipes and had rescued hundreds of cookbooks from church basement rummage sales.

Had Terry not blacked in the front windows, you'd be able to see Sagittarius Sunset, the rooftop restaurant in Vancouver's newest luxury hotel. Terry was there now, larger than life, overseeing the aftermath of Sunday brunch. Martha worked there too, as a waitress, but Sunday was her day off.

She went back into the kitchen, bent down and looked under the sink at the cleansers, sprays, waxes, polishes, and bottles of lemon oil. Cleaning the apartment was part of her arrangement with Terry, who charged her just fifty dollars a month for rent. She gathered what she needed on the counter, then turned to the dishes that filled the ancient porcelain sink, carefully washing the blue plates and wine glasses a friend of Terry's had brought back from Mexico.

The telephone rang.

She let it ring. Answering was usually trouble, people wanting Terry, wanting to know when he'd be back, impatient sometimes, hanging up abruptly, or leaving convoluted messages she might not get right. She rinsed the dishes. From the window over the sink she could see the sun winking in the windows of the houses in Kitsilano across the bay.

The telephone rang again. The glasses were now stacked neatly on a dishcloth beside the sink.

She was in no mood to speak with anyone, but the continuous ringing rattled her, so she picked up.

"It's me," Vito Bonello said in his nasal voice. "Did I wake you?"

"I just came in," she lied.

She could hear a truck grinding down a gear. He was pulled over by the road somewhere.

"So how's Terry been keeping?"

"He's fine."

"Is he still making them German tarts?"

Martha paused.

"Tortes," she said at length.

"Whatever," Vito said, adding, "Tell him 'hello' from me."

"I will."

"There might be some China white in the pipeline."

The line of shadow was creeping higher on the jagged mountains in the distance.

"Interested?"

"I can always use the bread."

"It'd have to be in the next few days."

"That would be fine. I've been planning a trip."

"What's the ___ for the trip?"

Part of what he'd said had gotten lost in the hiss of a truck's pneumatic brakes.

"Sorry. I didn't hear what you said."

"What's the occasion?"

"No occasion."

Neither of them spoke for a few seconds.

"You wanna be careful with the downers."

"I'm not on anything."

"You're just naturally a very subdued lady then," he said. "I'll be at the gallery tonight. We can talk."

•   •   •

For the longest time, she'd had no idea Terry was a dealer, or that Bonello was his main supplier. Terry's situation was ideal: he had a legitimate job, knew tons of people in Vancouver's arts community, made it a rule never to sell to anyone he didn't know well. Within a few days he could get you grass, hash, acid, smack (brown sugar or China white), plus all kinds of amphetamines. STP was big now. One day Terry might get busted, but so far his illicit career had been hassle-free, lucrative too. He had almost fifty thousand dollars in the bank, some of it in Canada Savings Bonds.

The Hong Kong smuggling syndicates that slip heroin into Vancouver hand it over to specialized subcontractors like Bonello, who, as Terry said, used maybe twenty different mules and liked to constantly vary his delivery routes. Sometimes he had it driven to Ontario, then taken by boat across the St. Lawrence at Prescott or Cornwall. The risk in that operation was getting across the prairies. RCMP detachments on the TransCanada have orders to stop and search cars with out-of-province plates. The quickest way to get heroin across the border was to mule it directly to Seattle.

As it happened, Martha was planning a trip to Portland. Her mother was in hospital again. The attack was serious this time. That's the impression Martha had gotten from Mrs. Tisdale. Her mother had suffered some kind of seizure while attending a conference in East Portland. They'd rushed her by ambulance to Multnomah County Hospital. A doctor there had run some tests and was talking about some kind of abnormality in her brain. An *edema*. That's the word Mrs. Tisdale had used.

The truth was her mother had been in hospital many times because of her lupus, flare-ups of the painful swelling and inflammation in her hips brought on by her drinking. Her mother was an alcoholic.

Martha didn't hold this against her, since she herself was a user of psychoactive substances to ward off her own blue moods and the panic attacks that were sometimes associated with them. She'd been living with the panic attacks for six years now, always thinking she'd gotten them under control until the next one caught her off guard.

At times she wondered if she was like her mother, if she was into pills the way her mother was into booze. Her mother's addiction to bourbon was probably symptomatic of deeper psychic turmoil. Unconscious rage at the cruelty of the world perhaps. And manic energy. Martha would never forget the day her father called her into the sunroom and talked like a psychiatrist, speaking about a clinical entity, manic depressive syndrome. She would never forgive him for his detached manner. If only he'd broken down, shown her something of his own pain.

Get over it. That's what her father would say if he knew about her panic attacks. Almost two months ago, Martha had freaked again, at work this time, a breezy day, the restaurant unusually quiet, no one out on the terrace. At loose ends, she'd strolled unthinkingly over to the edge to take in the view. The wall, reassuringly thick, perhaps two feet wide, came up higher than her waist. Grasping the iron slats cemented into the stone ledge, she was hardly in any danger. The skinniest child wouldn't fit between them. To throw yourself off, you'd have to climb onto the ledge, then shinny up and over the inward-curling fence.

It was the day after Labor Day, late in the afternoon, the office buildings across the street glowing in the September sun. Martha had peered down at the light dimming on the sidewalks below. It came on then, took her unawares. *You know you can't control it.* The pounding of her heart, crowding out all sound, blood pooling in her cheeks, her knees shaking, weakening, the silence crushing in on her as the fear took hold, her mind gripped by the thought she was going to — no, she had to — commit suicide. It was predetermined, given in everything around her, the haphazard procession of clouds, the irregular pattern of shadow on the mountains, the serene indifference of the sky above. The world held no place for her, and if that was so, what was she doing here? Her life so unwanted, so pointless . . . her death, the erasure of all consciousness, seemed imminent. It would be by her own hand. Or was it the imperturbable force of the world flowing through her? Her response to its unequivocal logic of absence and departure?

Within a matter of seconds, though it had felt like an eternity, Martha took possession of herself, turning away from the edge and the abyss beyond. She left work an hour early, tried to soothe herself by walking around the perimeter of Stanley Park, the sting of salt breeze vaguely comforting. *You can't run from it.*

It was nearly dark when she got home. *Your appetite goes.* She drank several cups of Buddha's Blend and forced herself to eat some peanut butter on a slice of dry bread. That evening, after several hours of yoga on the prayer rug, reciting half-remembered mantras from her stay on Hornby Island, she decided to go back on the antidepressants.

Since that day, she'd been okay at work. The world couldn't make you do things you didn't want to. Nothing pulled on her psyche from the panorama of space and sky, the office towers, the mountains in the distance, the impenetrable otherness of the clouds. It was unlikely she really wanted to kill herself, unlikely she'd ever jump onto that ledge, shinny up the slippery slats and throw herself over. The impulse was purely imaginary, she knew that, she told herself that, but her fear . . . her fear was real. Her heart pounded whenever she had to serve one of the tables near the spot where she'd looked out into the emptiness of all that space and felt the unforgiving randomness of the world. She made herself do it, knowing that the drowning silence happened when she ran from her fear. You lived knowing it could return at any time, but you didn't run.

The panic attacks weren't as bad as they'd once been. A few years ago, the sense of impending doom was such that she'd found it impossible to go for a walk alone in Stanley Park. A doctor had helped her a lot by telling her that if she turned away from her fear, it would grow. He'd also given her a name for her attacks. *Agoraphobia.* Agoraphobics, he said, couldn't handle situations that were open-ended. They needed boundaries, structure — the very things that had been missing in Martha's life. They especially needed work. He was right about that. Martha had always felt better whenever she'd worked. The routine of waitressing was therapeutic, there was comfort knowing other people expected something of you.

• • •

After hanging up from Bonello, Martha wondered if she should try the hospital again. Sunday probably wasn't a good day. Over the past week, she'd called twice but been unable to get any information about her mother. No use calling her father. Her parents hadn't spoken to each other for years, not since 1967 when her father had remarried, a flashy forty-year-old blonde named Jean Fogarty who owned a successful catering business in Portland. He'd just split, abandoning his only daughter, expecting her to look after herself *and* her mother, even though she was just thirteen, far too naive to realize her mother was crazy. That realization came in 1969, the year her mother went to Cuba for the sugar harvest.

Martha went back to cleaning the apartment, a solitary ritual, its pace and duration something she could control. She scrubbed the linoleum floor, dusted the baseboards, used a deluxe coat hanger fitted with a rag to dislodge the dust balls from between the ribs of the radiators. The oven was crusted with the spatter of filet mignon and pork roasts. She sprayed on a thick coat of oven cleaner, then put new foil around the burners on the stove. She opened the fridge — someone had put the clear plastic container of peanut butter on a shelf, without its lid. She found the lid under a newspaper on the kitchen table and put it back on. A few months ago, she'd come home from work and discovered Terry standing naked at the fridge, using a hair drier to melt the build-up of frost and ice in the freezer compartment, certain there were several tabs of acid buried in the ice.

The removal of dirt was not just satisfyingly predictable. It was artful. She took her time as she dusted the prints and photographs on the walls, the lamps, the bronze figurines from Thailand, the Chinese bowls. It sometimes took her five hours to do a thorough cleaning. The last thing she did was take the threadbare runners down to the street and pound them out with a broom.

• • •

It was nine by the time Martha had readied herself for the party. She looked out the kitchen window to get a sense of the weather, taking in the familiar shadowless black of the Pacific coast in late October. Her eyes were drawn to the lights across the bay in Kitsilano, the coldness of the night apparent in the piercing clarity of the red neon. In the hall closet, she found her green wool coat, the one she'd bought in Amsterdam years ago, still elegant though moths had gotten to the sleeves.

Waiting on the windblown sidewalk for the Powell Street bus, she turned the big collar up around her ears. The food stores along Denman were closed except for Cheung's and the 7-11. Across the street, a bearded man in a track suit stood pulling his ankle up to his buttock. He waved to her, then jogged slowly down the street toward Stanley Park. She had no idea who he was. A friend of Terry's? Someone she'd served in Sagittarius Sunset? A friendly stranger?

The bus dropped her in a rundown section of the east end, a block from the former knitting mill that now housed Crawl Straight, two floors of studios, workrooms, and a gallery run by an artists' cooperative. The co-op got money from the government because some of its members offered art therapy classes for the addicts and ex-convicts who lived in the halfway houses nearby.

Martha puffed her way up the creaky oak stairs to the gallery on the fourth floor, the syncopated throb of disco music growing louder — Terry called it New York fag music. Once inside the gallery, she let it happen, the hugging, the effusive greetings from people she vaguely knew, Terry's artist friends mostly.

These Sunday-night gatherings were a regular event for many of the waiters and waitresses who, like Martha, worked in the fancier restaurants around town. You weren't expected to say much. You could simply smile and pretend to listen. Watching the people around her converse, candlelight from the hurricane lamps atop the metal shelves flickering over their faces, she thought to herself these were great people, the best, they accepted you for who you were, they really didn't care what you did as long as it didn't bring them any harm. Except for one woman, a fat Hungarian sculptor known as Isabella the Terrible, an old art school friend of Terry's, who'd told Terry she was a flake, Terry laughing as he told her this, saying the one thing Isabella couldn't swallow was a pretty face.

The men, most of whom were gay, were fun to be around. They grinned and bopped to David Bowie, Freddie Mercury, and Marianne

Faithful, seldom saying much, the music far too loud for conversation. There were always new faces. A few weeks ago, she'd talked with a Gitane-smoking CPR conductor who was thinking about starting his own business in Montreal, importing Persian carpets. He'd wanted to sell her some cocaine. She smiled, recalling the quip about that particular habit being a cruel way of telling you you've got too much money.

She found an open bottle of Chablis on the counter, poured herself a glass, then went to inspect the offerings on the long metal table — oven trays of quail with roasted potatoes, grilled sausage and rack of lamb, barbecue ribs, the desiccated skeleton of a large salmon, several quiches and a marinated green bean and tomato salad, all of which had been part of Sunday brunch in some restaurant or other. Food didn't take her fancy, but she felt better with a drink in her hand. In the background, someone was saying that more rock groups had come out of Winnipeg than any other city in Canada. There were exuberant shrieks as new people arrived. By midnight, the stack of crested dinner plates was used up. If you arrived late and wanted food, you had to wash a plate. At some point, Terry came in, carrying an enormous Bavarian chocolate cream pie, which he proceeded to unwrap amid a chorus of oohs and aahs from the throng of leather-jacketed men.

Alcohol had mellowed her by the time she noticed Vito Bonello, oily even in candlelight and looking a little more thuggish than usual. She watched him greet the girls who hooked for him. One she recognized from Davie Street. Dark and petite, her nickname was Brenda Lee. And there was the one Terry called Mary Hartman, emaciated, with horribly acne-pitted cheeks. And the really ugly one who boasted she carried a knife in her boot.

It was after two when Vito came over and told her it was time they split. Terry shot her a quizzical look as she left. She beamed back a 'not-to-worry' smile. Being alone with Vito didn't frighten her. He was certainly capable of treachery and was probably a thug in certain situations, but he was easy to read. A big-boned Italian from Hamilton, Ontario, with a pot belly and a genuine fondness for Terry and his gay friends.

Leaving home young had made Martha streetwise. By the age of twenty-one, she'd lived, not exactly on, but near, the street in half a dozen American cities. Kept it more or less together in places that were like how you'd imagine Neil Young's burned-out basement. By the time she was thirty, she'd lived in Marrakesh, Kathmandu, Munich, and Brighton, England, getting to know lots of different people, and what she'd learned was that most people, even men as unorthodox as Terry and Vito, were predictable. Sometimes she knew what people were going to say even before they opened their mouth. Like Vito saying "colder than a witch's tit, eh?" as they hit the street.

They walked in silence, passing vacant lots and large red-brick warehouses, the light from the street lamps scattering in the windshields of the big rigs backed into the loading docks. It was a clear night, stars glinting in the black tapestry of the sky. As they turned down the side street where he'd parked, Vito put his arm around her shoulder, Martha not minding, thinking that being with people was sometimes a welcome distraction. They put boundaries around you, helped you forget the things that needed to be forgotten. About ten feet from his car, an innocuous Dodge Caravan, Vito stopped in his tracks, stuck four fingers in his mouth and whistled sharply. A yelping black dog, a Doberman puppy, bounded into the driver's seat and began turning around in excited circles, his front paws scraping at the windows and dashboard.

Vito opened the door and swatted the pup on the nose, sending him clambering into the back where he flopped down obediently on a fluffy white rug — polar bearskin, he boasted.

"Excuse the stink," he said as he yanked the ashtray overflowing with butts out of its rectangular hole in the dashboard and emptied it onto the street.

"That's better," he said as he turned the ignition, Martha rolling down the window, the stench of cigarettes less pungent than the whiffs of garlic and whiskey she was catching from his breath.

They drove the shore of Burrard Inlet, passing right by the Alberta Wheat Pool elevators, heading toward the docks, white lights strung along the fenced compounds, acres and acres of corrugated steel containers stacked on top of each other blocking their view of the water. After about ten minutes, they pulled up in front of a body shop. Vito stepped out, opened the chain-link gate, then hauled himself back in. He nosed the car into the yard, backing up into the shadows behind the body shop. From Vito's window, there was an unobstructed view of the choppy water.

"I'm looking after this property now. People pay me to drop their trash here and I arrange for its disposal."

Vito let the puppy out into the yard, Martha watching him sniff at a pile of rusty metal signs, then at scraps of drywall and the scatter of broken bricks and mortar. There were half a dozen storage sheds, windowless cubes of prefabricated aluminum resting on cinder-block foundations. Next to one of these sheds was an enamel stove, a pile of empty antifreeze jugs and a nest of black tubing.

"Joker owns this lot thought he could get away with brewing meth. Used them tubes to vent the fumes. He's doing a long stretch at Matsqui. First couple of years, cops kept coming to search the place. They've pretty much given up, it's just a junkyard now, everything's legit." He opened the car door and swung his heavy body out. "Well, just about everything."

She watched him pick his way through the debris to the shed, surprisingly agile for a big man. He disappeared for several minutes, then returned carrying a red tool box. He got back in the van beside her, not saying anything, holding the box on his lap for maybe ten seconds, squeezing the ends with his large hands. Then he clicked it open and took out three small packages wrapped in gauzy plastic.

"China white, ninety-percent pure. There's a huge demand for this shit in L.A. right now."

Martha stared at his thick nicotine-stained fingers, noticing the matted black hair below the knuckles. She waited for him to continue.

"Bags are vacuum-sealed."

He made as if he was going to hand the merchandise over, then drew back. "Here's the deal," he said. "You get across the border. Right?"

"Right." She didn't like to think about that part of it.

"Someone'll meet you at the Venezia, it's a restaurant out in the Seattle Center, you know, the old fair grounds, you can't miss it."

He rolled down his window several inches. The puppy was parading up and down by the embankment, now and then raising a leg and sprinkling the fence.

"They serve great eggplant sandwiches, the Venezia's a bona fide pasta restaurant, the only place I'd eat at out there. Sit at a table on the patio. Wear something red in your hair."

He handed her a Nordstrom's shopping bag. "Put the packages in the bottom of this bag. Your contact will take it from you."

"That's it? A straight drop-off?"

"That's right. No suitcase of cash for you to disappear with . . . ." He pulled out a roll of bills from his trouser pocket. "Here's a hundred dollars. For your expenses. You get six more when you get back. I'm good for it."

"I want a thousand this time."

He laughed and pounded the steering wheel with the fleshy edge of his hands, his fingers curled into half-fists. "Hey, it's not like I couldn't find someone else. Mules are cheap in this economy. You're a spunky lady, a nice lady too. So I'll throw in another hundred. But that's it. Take it or leave it."

"I'll take it . . . . Terry thinks I'm worth a grand."

"Terry's a fruit-loop. What's he know?"

He handed her the packages.

It was arranged. Nothing more needed to be said.

Time suddenly slowed down. Without even glancing at Vito's pockmarked face, she could sense the need buried in his lifeless brown eyes, and the pride, always close to the surface, so fragile in a man of action.

He fiddled with the radio, then moved over and put his arm around her.

Avoiding his eyes, she looked through the windshield at the rise of land on the far side of Burrard Inlet.

"Don't you find me attractive?"

"That's a loaded question." The flickering of lights across the water was mesmerizing.

"I got a right to ask it, though."

"It's nothing personal, believe me."

"I'm nice to you, aren't I?"

"Vito, if sex is part of the deal, you can find someone else."

"You're touchy tonight."

"If it makes you feel any better, I haven't been with anybody for a long, long time."

"Why's that?"

"I don't know," she paused. "I haven't felt like it."

"Well, we can't have that," he said, rubbing her cheek with his thick fingers. "What'll put you in the mood?"

"Vito, I'm serious."

"All right. All right."

They sat in silence for several minutes, Martha smelling his sour cigarette breath, the reek of his clothes, thinking to herself, each day was different, there was no fixed destination in her life.

"Okay. I'll drive you home," he said at length. "I won't even ask you for a blow job."

Martha smiled to herself. Had Vito asked the question seriously, had he insisted on sex, actually taken his penis out of his trousers, she would've sucked him. In fact, the thought of it was beginning to arouse her. The one thing she'd learned about herself over the years was that she was attracted to strong men, men with big egos, men who didn't count on her to prop them up. She had enough trouble keeping herself on track, thank you very much. She didn't need another person's insecurities.

At a traffic light opposite the marina near the entrance to Stanley Park, she rolled down the window all the way to listen to the tinkle of the chimes on the mast wires. Orange lights flickered on the Lion's Gate Bridge in the distance. It was not yet dawn, but there was a blue tinge to the sky above the trees near the point.

They crossed town to the English Bay side of the park, the car's headlights tracking the path by the water. A helmeted man in a bright yellow jersey sped by on a racing bicycle, red reflectors rotating fast on the wheels. It occurred to her briefly that she might reach over and put her hand on Vito's thigh, change the direction of things, but she let the thought die. She almost never took the initiative. Never needed to.

Vito pecked her cheek before letting her off in front of Svenson's Ice Cream Parlour, a plastic jack-o'-lantern blinking in the window. Denman Street was eerily quiet. The bag lady who sits on the stone steps of the Ukrainian church had gone to wherever it was she went in the dead of night. Martha encountered no one as she walked the half block to her apartment, the crinkly packages of white powder stuffed into her shoulder bag.

SEATTLE

The smell of bacon grease was seeping up between the broken floorboards in the hall. Martha opened the kitchen window, then cut a banana into sour yogurt, but could only swallow a few mouthfuls. Looking out at the gray mist settling over the city, she tried to discern some meaning in the blank surfaces of things. Beleaguered by doubt, she wished Terry was still there to distract her, but he'd left for work over an hour ago. She couldn't really turn back now, her canvas duffel bag already packed, the packages of heroin fitted into a blue box of tampons, the box wrapped up tightly inside her amber shawl.

In the bathroom, she considered her hair. It was naturally tinged with red. People sometimes assumed she was from Quebec. She parted it in the middle, then drew it back in two wings which she clipped with barrettes. It was, she hoped, an athletic all-American look. She dropped the comb into a black leather purse containing her money and passport, her mascara and lipstick, her prescription Zoloft and Ativan and some Percocets and Valiums which Terry had gotten for her. The last thing she slipped into the purse was the paperback from her night table, a trashy biography of Janis Joplin.

It occurred to her, while she waited for the taxi, that she was hopelessly irresponsible. It was depressing to realize she had no education to speak of, except for that awful year at the University of Colorado when she'd had to drop out of her courses in philosophy. *You can only drift for so long*. Her father had said that. *Your money or your life*. An old boyfriend had said that. Somehow Martha had reached the age of thirty-six without worrying about money. But those days were definitely over. Not a week went by she didn't wonder how much money was left in her mother's trust fund. Like most children born into once-wealthy families, she'd lived her life expecting there'd be some money for her. Now she wasn't so sure. That's why she'd begun to think about going back to school to study graphic arts or photography. Unless she acquired a marketable skill of some kind, she'd be waitressing for the rest of her life. After a few drinks though, she'd feel less worried about the future and she'd tell herself there was nothing so wrong with being a thirty-six-year-old waitress. Besides, it was good to be inured to the precariousness of human arrangements. *It doesn't matter how long you live, all that matters is how you live the time you have. Don't waste it worrying about money or the silly things money buys.* Wasn't that so? Her mother believed it was.

At the sound of honking from the street, Martha grabbed her duffel bag and purse, locked the door and rushed down to the waiting taxi, seeing Nick's sister at the cash register and catching a glimpse of Nick himself, sleeves rolled up, tending to something on the grill. In the back seat of the taxi, she watched the rainwater bead on the windows. There was no one she knew among the customers in the delicatessen and bakery across the street. A boy was taking a tray of cookies out of a minivan. What light there was on the street swam off the headlights of the other cars, making the day seem monochromatic somehow. It could rain for weeks. Besieged by the lack of sunlight, people sometimes overdosed, anything to break the monotony.

At the Greyhound Terminal, Martha joined the lineup for tickets, standing behind two teenaged boys in army surplus jackets. From their conversation she gathered they were on their way to Mexico. She remembered how carefree her life had been when she was their age. After leaving the pink house in the Castro, back when San Francisco was still affordable, she'd set her sights on seeing the world, had lived for a time in Marrakesh, crossed Afghanistan, holed up in Freak Street, Kathmandu, for over a year, then gotten sick and retraced her steps. She'd done a stint as a waitress in Brighton, England, another stint as a waitress in Boulder — that was after she'd dropped out of university, getting hooked on cheap brown sugar, buying it from one of the cooks in the restaurant at the wholesale price of seven dollars for one-tenth of a gram, less than half the street price.

In Boulder, she'd allowed many men into her life — men who'd said she was special, her very presence in the world an extraordinary thing. Married men had treated her to fancy dinners, then baffled her by the urgency of their need for sex. In the last few years, she'd come to realize she was just an ordinary woman, and this realization had helped. Since the abortion, she no longer needed a man in her life, she was better without one. For she'd discovered that the panic attacks were always worse when things got serious with a man.

At the front of the line now, Martha asked for a one-way ticket to Seattle, the ticket agent's face a blur behind the rippled yellow glass partition. She browsed for a while in the souvenir shop, thumbing through the paperbacks on the swivel rack. Then she went out and sat down on a bench in the waiting room. She tried to read the paperback in her purse, but couldn't, the writer's interview with a high-school teacher who'd known Janis Joplin as a teenager in Port Arthur, Texas, nothing of that world floating up from the black print on the book's pink-edged pages, the meaning of the words not even registering in her mind.

A fat man in a stained raincoat, a battered suitcase on his lap, sat across from her, muttering to himself.

"Late as usual," he said to no one in particular. "Nobody cares to be on time nowadays."

"Bye-bye, missy," he said when she got up to go to the ladies' room, a look of bewilderment on his face, Martha guessing that this waiting room was his home during the day.

Someone had scratched the name Whiskey Tess on the side of the toilet stall. It was soothing to look at the world up close: the doodles, smudges, and chipped paint on the partition, the stains and scuff marks on the white floor tiles, the weave of her sweater, even the texture of the skin on the back of her hand.

At the sink, she ran the water until it was drinkably cold, then swallowed a white angel. She liked the effect that Valium had on her. Such a great body drug. She'd seem naturally groggy at the border, wouldn't betray any nervousness to the authorities. Vito had told her she didn't fit the profile of the drug mule, the hippie with an ounce of grass maybe, but they weren't hassling the small stuff at the border any more. No percentage in it.

At noon, she went out to the platform and joined the line waiting to board the bus. Twenty minutes later, they pulled out into the confusion of Davie Street. For some reason, the round Polaroid windows didn't open. The stench of air freshener wafting up from the toilet at the back, and a sickly damp smell that was definitely mold of some kind, perhaps from the foam used in the construction of the seats, made her feel like vomiting. She sensed panic massing at the back of her mind, but the Valium kept it in check.

Fog blanketed the valley. For a while, all she could see were the trunks of trees near the shoulder. Every now and then, a transport truck thundered by on the opposite side of the divided highway. Occasionally she glimpsed the sprawl of tract housing and a shopping mall. Here was a world in which people went to jobs as sales managers and occupational therapists, came home and drove their children to ballet lessons and hockey practices. Here it wasn't the early seventies any more.

At the border, everyone got off the bus. The lights were on in the U.S. Customs and Immigration building, uniformed men and women milling around inside. Martha joined the clump of passengers waiting for the driver to remove the bags from the luggage compartment. Eventually her duffel bag landed on the wet pavement. She slung it over her shoulder and followed the others to the entrance to the government building. Thanks to the Valium, she was nicely slowed up, resigned to whatever might happen, though getting busted had almost no reality in her mind.

Mist hung over the ridge of pine forest on the far side of the building. The boys in the army surplus jackets were far ahead of her in the line, already at the customs counter, removing everything from their knapsacks, then unrolling their sleeping bags on the counter. She could see two male officers saying something, giving instructions. One of the officers was dangling what looked like a bag of apples in his hand. *You can't control what happens.*

Ten minutes later, it was her turn. She handed her passport to a stocky man with a chin dimple.

"How long have you been out of the country?" He punched her name into a computer.

"Since August."

"Where do you live, Miss?"

"Vancouver."

"What do you do there?"

"I live with my boyfriend."

He looked at her carefully. "What work do you do?"

"I . . . I'm a waitress."

He nodded and smiled.

He was older than she'd thought at first, the kind of man who would feel it was his responsibility to protect a woman traveling alone. For a crazy second she felt like confessing to him what her duffel bag contained.

"Where are you headed today?"

"Portland."

"Who will you be staying with in Portland?"

"My father," she lied.

"Will you be returning to Canada?"

"Yes."

"What's the purpose of your visit?"

"My mother's in hospital."

"Which one?"

"Multnomah County."

"I bet that's a good hospital," he said, handing her an orange slip. "Good luck."

She had made it through. An officer collected the slip she'd been given, waving her out of the swinging glass doors into the United States. The bus had been driven forward, the sleek greyhound leaping across the back window making her smile, its familiar presence a source of relief, a benign statement about the world. She placed her duffel bag in the luggage compartment and got back on board.

Soon they were on their way again. She sank back in her seat and took in the world's obdurate presence, sun breaking through low gray clouds, bales of hay dotting the pastures, the black and white cows grazing under the autumn light.

A memory of Jon flooded her mind. In Boulder, when she was really down in the dumps, he'd convinced her to accompany him to Hornby Island, to a holiness commune founded by a number of Buddhists, Americans mostly. The island was in the Strait of Georgia. She'd fallen in love with the high ridge of land where the community had built an ashram entirely out of cedar shakes.

But her relationship with Jon hadn't been secure enough to withstand communal life. He'd insisted on sleeping with other women, declaring the experience a necessary element in his "journey of self discovery." Usually she was the one who ended romantic relationships, quickly sensing their impossibility, leaving before being left, protecting herself from unwanted feelings of abandonment that way. Jon's betrayal had caught her off guard. Prayer was of no help. In fact she found the daily meditation sessions a little grueling. Perhaps if she hadn't been pregnant, hadn't had that abortion, her second, things might've turned out differently with Jon. Quite a few people had since told her they would've preferred she be the one who stayed.

She might still be at the commune had she not met Terry about a month after the abortion. They'd slept together the first night. Afterward Terry admitted he was mostly gay, but could still get turned on by masculine women. She had not taken this as a compliment. Her strongly veined hands, it turned out, were her chief masculine feature. They weren't good as lovers, but they did like each other a lot. He made her see how stupid it was to stay in the commune if it didn't mean anything to her. She ended up crashing at his apartment for a week. Something in her must have charmed him because he invited her to stay permanently. Over the past year they'd worked out a modus vivendi. He ignored her blue moods, playfully scolding her for not grabbing life by the throat, and she wasn't in the least put off by the emaciated drag queens he occasionally brought home.

Waking from her reverie, Martha noticed the bus was now inching along in the clog of Seattle's rush-hour traffic, sun blasting off the windows of the suburban houses built in tiers on the hills that lined the shore. She had to squint to see the choppy waters of Puget Sound. When they stopped moving, she figured there was an accident or construction on the road ahead. The air in the bus, already saturated with the toilet's acrid air freshener, was now lousy with someone's farts, prompting the two women in the seat behind her to giggle nervously.

There were cheers when they finally pulled into the terminal. They all bunched in around the side of the bus, waiting for a muscular Indian to unload the luggage. Grabbing her duffel bag off the ground, Martha made her way into the waiting room, its shabbiness a shock after the clean public spaces she'd grown used to north of the border. She tried to get a sense of what was going on. Gum, cigarette smoke and the smell of something rank confused the room. A fat white woman was reining in a three-year-old boy and holding a squalling baby in her lap. The baby was the source of the rank smell. Half a dozen people were lined up in front of the pay telephones.

Martha made her way down a corridor to the women's washroom; a mesh barrier, with a red metal sign, ENTRY BY TOKEN ONLY, forced her to retrace her steps. She cast around for the machine that dispensed tokens, her concentration broken by a commotion on the far side of the room, people getting up out of their seats, moving away from a scrawny Indian who was jabbering at them, gesticulating angrily, pointing at the mesh-covered windows above the ticket counter, sensing some danger up there, a sniper with a loaded gun perhaps.

At that point, Martha decided to forego the washroom, ducking outside where it was cool and there was a line of taxis. She got into the first car. It wouldn't be a long ride, the Pacific Emerald wasn't far. It wasn't the Hilton, but it was supposed to be safe. There was also Odin's Inn and the St. Regis, they were a little nicer, Terry said, but the musicians who crashed there were cokeheads.

They drove through a part of Seattle that was still seedy, buildings boarded up or given over to liquor stores, porn shops, topless bars. Gulls and pigeons roosted on the horizontal struts of the billboards.

The driver was checking her out in the rearview mirror. A scruffy man in a red baseball cap.

He braked hard for a light, sending her sliding forward on the seat.

"Sorry about that."

They rocketed past a derelict warehouse, the plywood slabs in the windows covered with posters that said READ DIANETICS BY L. RON HUBBARD, Martha thinking to herself, people in need of faith got screwed by those keen to provide it. *Pay attention to your anxiety. Your body's telling you something, pain's essential for spiritual growth.* Jon was so smug, such a power tripper.

"Your hotel's down there," the driver said. "It's one way, so I'll have to take the next one."

She glanced down the side street, saw traffic lights hanging from thick cables at the bottom of a steep incline. Halfway down the hill, after they'd veered a little to the right, the Pacific Emerald Hotel loomed into view, its stone facade blackened by years and years of rainy weather.

The driver let her off on the deserted sidewalk in front of the hotel. She picked up her bag, glancing toward the entrance, not sure what to expect, certainly not a doorman. She gazed down the hill toward the bay, not a soul in sight, then looked up at the windows on the upper floors of the hotel.

Once the taxi had driven off, she went into the lobby. Old men were gathered around tables, playing cards, with the periodic *thawk-thwack* of the cards slamming down on a table signifying the end of a round.

The young male clerk at the desk nodded obligingly when she said she needed a room for two nights.

"You're in luck. I have a room with a view of the bay."

The clerk had done something to his hair, it was orange.

"Where ya'll from?" he asked as she began to fill out the registration card. "Not that it's really my business."

"Canada," she said. "I'm heading south. I've got family in Oregon." She wanted to create a normal impression, didn't want the young man to think she was down on her luck, a floozy or a nutcase, though she knew he wouldn't have cared one way or another. He had his own life to worry about. Boundaries existed between people, otherwise there would be no freedom.

"There's one thing I need to ask you to do," the clerk said. "That's to drop off your keys at the desk when you go out. It's part of the new security system we're trying out."

"Of course."

"Not that this is a dangerous part of town, but we've had problems with guests getting drunk and whatnot, then losing their keys out on the street." He gestured toward the geezers playing cards. "It's quite a problem, especially when the keys get into the wrong hands. That's why we like to keep them all here." He handed her the key to her room. "One other thing. We lock the front doors at eleven, but there'll be someone here at the desk to buzz you in. There should be someone. If there's not, you wait, I guess," he laughed. "Just kidding. The night guy's never away from the desk for more than ten minutes." He laughed again. "I hope."

That the hotel was once elegant was apparent from the brass plate and the sculpted plaster cornices around the elevator doors. There was a rich mauve glow from the conch-shaped wall sconces. Upholstered chairs, worn in spots so the stuffing was visible, had been pushed up against the walls, along with an assortment of chrome chairs and what looked like plastic footstools, recreation-room furniture from the fifties. It wasn't really a place for the budget-conscious business traveler. What it was was a welfare hotel, exactly what she wanted, a single room with bath for $19.95 plus state tax.

Martha stepped into the elevator and put her thumb on the black button. Nothing happened. She pressed it again. Still nothing. She pressed the button once more, harder this time. The elevator lurched to life and rose haltingly, Martha holding her breath as she listened to the inconstant groan of its motor, the pulleys and cables clanking in the shaft. She got off on the seventh floor, went the wrong way in the dim corridor, then retraced her steps. Some of the metallic numbers on the doors were missing, new numbers had been sloppily inked in with a felt marker. Passing an open door, she glimpsed a shirtless man lying on a bed, a can of beer in his hand.

At the end of the corridor, she let herself into a sizeable room, light flooding in from south- and west-facing windows. The walls were cracked, cratered from moisture, and the paint was chipped, revealing a mottled peach that matched the frayed taffeta bedspread. She dropped her duffel bag onto an armchair, thinking at first someone had left a pink and yellow handkerchief on the back. On closer inspection, it turned out to be an antimacassar sewn into the fabric.

From the west-facing window, she could see the peaks of the Olympics camped in the hazy light across the bay. The view more than made up for the garishness of the furnishings. There was a distant roar of traffic. She peered down, saw where it was coming from — a busy freeway disappearing and reappearing in the gaps between the nearby office buildings. Wasn't there something weird about this freeway? She remembered what it was — traffic lanes were reversed for the morning and evening rush hours. She looked at her watch. A quarter after five. Hundreds of miles to the south, they'd be bringing her mother's meal tray, the last light of the day streaking into the hospital room. She let the sadness of this thought take her, knowing there was no way she could hammer it down into her unconscious.

In the bathroom, she ran the water at the sink, washing down a white angel, taking care not to touch her lips to the faucet. It was only her second of the day. Waiting for it to take effect, she returned and stood by the window. The sun had dipped down behind the mountains, though the signs of its existence were still evident in the kaleidoscopic transformations taking place in the darkening panorama it had left behind. Wispy pink clouds sailed across the near sky, gathering in the haze above the bay, then getting lost in the distant glow of rose as they moved west. A ribbon of purple was stitched all along the horizon where the mountains and sky melded.

Martha felt the breeze shivering in toward her from the choppy waters of Elliott Bay. For perhaps half an hour she waited for the blackness, chanting to herself, whispering to the Mister Sun of her childhood, not knowing what to make of all the vacancy in the world. It took her a while to get her feelings under control and put her mind to work on the problem of going out for something to eat.

When she did finally get downstairs, the lobby was deserted except for a solitary man hunched over one of the tables gathering up a bunch of crumpled lottery tickets, stuffing them into the folds of his worn wallet. All the action had moved to the beverage room where it was happy hour, half-price draft beer every day of the week between five and seven.

Outside on the sidewalk, she considered heading down the hill to the water's edge, wanting the solace there, curious to witness from the ground what she'd seen from her room. But it was dark now, and her greater need was for food. So she turned the other way, trekking up several steep blocks toward the shopping district, proceeding from memory, the street ridiculously quiet, almost surreal, the funky little clothing and crafts stores closed, grates pulled across the windows. She passed Dimitri's, a Greek restaurant, its blue neon sign flickering in the window. For some reason, it made her think of the most expensive entrée at Sagittarius Sunset, something called the carpetbagger — a thick filet mignon steak with a pocket carved out in the center for oysters in a garlic sauce. It wasn't a popular dish and Terry was thinking of taking it off the menu.

It was necessary to cut through the business district to get to the fast-food strip which was, if she remembered correctly, near one of the northerly entrances to the freeway. Farther out than she'd thought. Twenty, perhaps thirty, minutes went by before she reached a six-lane highway, everything floodlit and impossibly bright, gas stations, car washes, transmission shops, discount emporiums selling mattresses and broadloom. But no McDonalds, Pizza Huts, or Taco Bells, just Archie's Place, a sleazy diner, its windows tinted and smudged so you couldn't see in.

The glare of headlights seared her eyes. Occasionally motorists honked. She was on the verge of turning back when a Dairy Queen sign perched on stilts in the distance caught her eye. It would have to do.

"Hi, ma'am, what'll it be?" asked the dolled-up teenager behind the counter. "We have a special on pumpkin shakes."

"A banana split."

"It'll take a minute or so."

She waited in the hard bright light, thinking to herself that the customers she served in Sagittarius Sunset tipped her well, even though she didn't smile like this girl. She didn't require her customers to act as if they were having fun, she didn't make them feel something was wrong with them if they weren't really positive about the meal.

Martha inspected the concoction in front of her, scraped away the chocolate syrup, pushed aside the crushed nuts, popped the maraschino cherry into her mouth, thinking at least the bananas were a source of potassium. As she ate, an image of her mother's ramshackle cottage came into her mind. She'd once contemplated moving in, helping out by doing the shopping. But she'd been unable to follow through. It was mostly her mother's drinking, seeing her like that, in her torn housecoat and shabby slippers, face slightly bloated, hair unkempt, dipping oatmeal cookies into her bourbon and raspberry seltzer.

On her last visit, Martha had noticed her mother was unsteady on her legs, her ankles puffy from all the cortisone they'd pumped her full of. The only food in the cottage consisted of packaged goods, snacky things you could get at by pulling a carton or box out of the refrigerator. She'd tried to get her mother to eat more healthily, encouraged her to cook brown rice, carrots, broccoli, various kinds of beans.

The worst was that for several years now her mother had been having trouble keeping track of things. She'd get lost driving into Portland for her bridge games with the Laurelhurst gang. It was a good thing Horst and Ulrike Maar were down the road and could deliver firewood from Tillamook and do whatever chores needed to be done.

• • •

It had begun to drizzle, the swishing of tires on the wet pavement vaguely menacing. To avoid the glare of lights on the highway, Martha had taken another route back to the hotel, a less busy road that seemed to run parallel to the highway, but at some point must have veered in the wrong direction. She found herself not far from the bus terminal, on a street of porn shops and liquor stores, litter and broken glass on the sidewalk. Two men in baseball caps conversing in front of the Wahkiakam Mission hollered something as she went by, then began following her.

In Vancouver she would've thought nothing of it, but this was an American city. She quickened her pace, setting her sights on an orange crane in the distance. Thankfully, lots was happening on the street, plenty of men in hooded sweatshirts and tattered jean jackets loitering outside the bars and all-night coffee shops. She knew she was on the right track when she passed the abandoned building with the READ DIANETICS BY L. RON HUBBARD signs in the windows. And there was that used clothing store and the Seafarers International Union Hall. After a little while, she was out of the flattened-out skid row, pretty much alone on the steeper streets of the shopping district. At the Masonic Temple, she glanced back, saw that the men were still behind her.

She walked as fast as she could, head down, arms swinging. A block or so farther on, a car pulling out of an underground parking lot passed a few feet in front of her, startling her. She began to run, she pretended she was a jogger, though she wasn't dressed for it, running for perhaps ten minutes, slowing down only when she got to the narrow street of camera shops and designer clothing boutiques she'd driven down in the taxi earlier that day. She looked back again. The men were no longer there. She stopped to catch her breath, sucking in the cool fresh air coming up from the bay. Then she hurried on, her own footsteps the only sound she heard on the last steep block before she got to the Pacific Emerald.

The lobby was quiet, just two or three tables of old men playing cards in the mauve light. She picked up her key at the front desk and took the elevator up to the seventh floor, less troubled than before by its jerky motion. The corridor was noisier now, the splatter of TV gunfire and the nasal twang of a country-and-western song coming at her from different directions. An old man in baggy trousers and an undershirt stood in a doorway babbling to himself, impossible to make complete sense of what he was saying, something about having bet his bundle on a horse of a different color. He brilled out what he had to say, then slammed the door, a brain-cracking thud. His tirade continued, muffled behind the closed door.

Life has a definite undertow, she thought as she let herself into her room. People got caught in it and ended up here. Without flicking on the lights, she drew the safety latch, slipped out of her jeans and sweater, then got into bed. Ignoring the occasional burst of men's laughter from the room above, she listened for the shrieking of the gulls over the bay, audible now and then above the whir of machinery coming from the roof of a nearby building. After a while, feeling a draft from the windows, she got up and spread her coat on the bed. A few minutes later, she got up again and checked her duffel bag to make sure the packages of heroin were still there. Then she shook out a couple of Ativan from the plastic bottle and slipped them under her tongue, trusting they would efficiently cloud her mind and bring on sleep.

THE ROOF

Shrill laughter from the corridor woke her out of a dreamless sleep. She splashed cold water on her face, put on some eye shadow and clipped back her hair with red barrettes. From the window, she saw that fog had settled over the coast. The flat roofs of the warehouses by the wharf were just discernible, but the harbor was gone, so too were the roads, though she could hear the rumble of traffic below. A truck was straining to climb a hill a few blocks away.

She stuffed the gauze packages into the bottom of the Nordstrom bag, as Vito had instructed, and went out. Nearby, at Amy's Snack Bar, she sat at a white formica counter and lingered over a bran muffin and several cups of chicory-flavored coffee. To kill some time, she took a stroll along the waterfront, now a funky neighborhood of fringe theaters and art galleries. She vaguely remembered this part of town from years ago, when she'd driven up with some of her mother's friends for an anti-war rally. Her mother would be thrilled to know Rosie the Riveter's was still going strong, the works of Karl Marx, Mao Tse-tung and Fidel Castro, in their familiar pale-yellow Peking editions, on display in the dusty front window. Recommended reading for November, according to a handwritten sign, was Ernest Mandel's *Late Capitalism* and Nick Salvatore's biography of Eugene Victor Debs. Her eye happened on a used paperback copy of Germaine Greer's *The Female Eunuch*, such a strange cover — a molded body suit resembling a woman's torso hanging from a horizontal bar, suspended in darkness, the torso tallowy and stiff, with handles on the hips. It was a book she'd been unable to finish. Raw experience was what she was after in those days. If only she'd been more interested in ideas, she would've gotten on better with her mother and might've even agreed to enroll in sociology at Portland State.

An hour or so before it was time, Martha made her way to the monorail station at 4th and Pine, stepping into a spotlessly clean car filled with voluble Japanese tourists. The loudspeaker issued a warning to stand clear of the doors, then the train screeched to life, tunneling through the fog on automatic pilot, heat blasting from metal grills beneath the seats.

Out at the fairgrounds, it was cooler and a little forlorn, the souvenir and concession stands closed for the season. The olympic-sized pool had been drained, the blue basin scattered with leaves and litter. Workmen in overalls were dismantling a carousel, carrying brightly painted horses up a ramp into an orange moving van.

Martha made her way over to the James Polk Memorial Crafts Center and Food Court, a corrugated metal building that looked more like a defunct airplane hangar than a gathering place for sightseers and shoppers. She stood on the mezzanine-floor balcony and peered down at the crowd below. There'd just been an event of some kind, a meeting with speeches and perhaps prayers. Elderly men and women wearing name tags were milling around rows of folding chairs.

Neon signs buzzed at the edges of the mezzanine and main floors. Flaming reds for burgers and corned beef sandwiches, pinks and yellows for cookies and waffles, tropical greens and blues for sweets and ice cream. You could get flavored popcorn, onion rings, Chinese spring rolls, Caesar salads, fried chicken, apple and cherry strudels, roasted nuts, fudge, Belgian chocolates, Eskimo pies and frozen Oreo-cookie bars. Terry would find all this, the sheer volume of fast food, incredibly vulgar. But you couldn't blame the people shuffling by, they were making the best of what there was. Perhaps there was something sad and a little shameful about the place, but you still had to admire the folks, tourists most of them, they'd worked all their lives in some bleak factory town and were now seeing some of the country before their health gave out.

The Venezia Restaurant was at the Mercer Street end of the main floor. An enclosed building within the food court. Italian bunting above the shuttered windows and swinging saloon door. There was a little patio out front, made private on two sides by a high wooden trellis decorated with faux ivy. Ten or twelve tables with red-and-white checked tablecloths. As instructed, Martha sat down at one of these.

"Jeez, am I stupid," a woman nearby said. "I left my coupons at home."

"Too late now," her companion shrugged, holding the check in her hand, counting out dollar bills.

No sign of a waiter.

Martha stood up and looked through the window into the restaurant, glimpsing a mural on the wall, a bridge over a canal in a place that was unmistakably Venice.

A pimply boy in a gondolier's hat waved and came out to take her order.

Sipping her cappuccino, Martha was gripped by a familiar sensation, the anticipation of something new, the uncertainty that comes when you don't know what will happen next. She took note of the fat man several tables away. Dressed in plaid trousers and a team jacket that said Al on the sleeve, he began cracking the knuckles of his swollen white hands, scowling at his wife. "I just hope we don't get ripped off," he said in a loud voice.

There was always that fear, Martha thought. It was what some people feared more than anything else. Watching the couples file by, often with an ice-cream cone or some sweet thing in their leathery hands, she was reminded of the stories her mother used to tell about life in the Tillamook woods during the hungry times after the stock market crashed in '29 — folks survived then by shooting coyotes for bounty money, poaching salmon, and picking berries by the bushel.

She saw him coming. It had to be him. A short stocky man in a cheap suit. Wavy dark hair and a well-trimmed goatee. Their eyes locked, but he continued past her, tossing a styrofoam cup into the waste bin. His unguarded smile threw her off, for a crazy instant she wondered if he was just someone trying to pick her up. Then he turned around and came back.

"I didn't keep you waiting, did I?"

She shook her head.

"You're better-looking than Vito said you'd be."

The shopping bag was on the chair beside her. He glanced at it and grinned.

"Been shopping, I see."

He didn't look like anyone you'd meet in Vancouver.

"You got nothing to worry about now."

He smelled of garlic, one of his teeth was capped in gold.

"So, what's it like up there in Canada?"

"Do you mean the weather?

"Sure, the weather."

"Rainy, actually."

"You like it?"

"It's all right."

"There's worse places?"

"I guess."

"Where are you staying?"

"With some friends of mine."

"Your friends like to party?"

"I don't think so. Not tonight anyway."

There was a moment of silence. A dozen or so round-faced men walked by, Korean sailors from one of the ships in port, probably on their way to the Space Needle.

At one time, she might have said she wanted to party, might have gone with him, unmindful of the danger, the likelihood there'd be drugs and friends of his, guys in the mob, who'd consider her fair game. She was older now, no longer oblivious to the risk of bad endings.

"This looks like a fun place, if you're a granddad or a grandma, that is," he said facetiously, studying the folks strolling past the table. "Can I tell you something? Seattle's not a lot of fun for a fella like me. It's all business here. Everyone jogs and works for Microsoft. Aren't any nightclubs or all-night poker games. I miss Vegas, I'll tell you that . . . Do you know Vegas?"

"No," she said, glancing at the fat man still cracking his knuckles.

"So how's Vito?"

"He's fine," she said. "I saw him a few days ago."

"Vito still have a problem keeping his pecker in his pants?"

"I wouldn't know."

"Well, tell him hello from me. Will you be sure to do that?"

"I will."

She looked up, saw the waiter talking to someone in the gloom just inside the swinging door.

"You're a nice-looking chick. Sure you don't want to party?"

"I've got plans. I really do. But thank you for the offer."

"You can't blame a guy for trying."

"No. Of course not," she said, avoiding his eyes.

"You know something. You're a little different. I mean for a mule. Which sort of makes you perfect for the job, doesn't it?"

"I guess."

"You're not doing this for the money, I'll bet. It's the thrills, am I right?"

"No. It's the money, actually."

"The money, huh? You hold down a straight job that doesn't pay you enough to get high, huh?"

It dawned on her that he was trying to figure out if she was one of Vito's hookers. "I'm a waitress," she said, telling herself to be careful. There were things it'd be better this guy didn't know.

"That's what I thought. Vito never asked you to hook for him, I'll bet . . . you're not mean enough . . . a girl needs a killer instinct in that line of work. You gotta figure that men who need to pay for it, they're either psycho or they're just pathetic . . . I'm not upsetting you, am I?"

"No," she said, sensing he was trying to upset her, remembering another man, an architect she'd gone out with in Boulder, who'd come on to her by being deliberately outrageous.

Right then, there was a quick burst of light. She looked up, saw a second group of Korean sailors, five or six stragglers traipsing by, one of them had just used his camera, taken a shot, it wasn't clear of what.

A harmless intrusion, but it was enough to set things rolling.

Her companion abruptly stood up.

"Well, I gotta get back," he said. "It sure was nice talking to you."

With that remark, he picked up the shopping bag and disappeared into the throng of people shuffling through the food court.

• • •

The China white was on its way to a mob lab somewhere to get diluted, packaged, and distributed to low-level dealers like Terry. And she was seven hundred dollars richer. Or at least she would be when she got back to Vancouver.

With her job over, Martha ought to have felt relieved, but an uneasy feeling tracked her as she left the fairgrounds, crossing Denny Way, then meandering through a poor neighborhood, clapboard houses with plastic sheeting over the windows and rotting front porches. In the shadow of an elevated section of highway, a white man in a maroon track suit was pivoting twenty feet from a rusty basketball hoop, taking a long shot, while two black teenagers stood off to one side, kicking at the asphalt. Farther away, three young men sat on a bleacher, passing around a joint.

At a corner grocery not far from the hotel, Martha picked up several cartons of apple juice and half a dozen little boxes of raisins. Inspecting the rack of snack foods, she remembered how she'd made herself sick on salty snacks as a teenager. Always such an assortment to choose from: tortilla chips, nachos, corn chips, bacon and cheddar fries, pretzels, cheese popcorn, and potato chips of different flavors, barbecue, sour cream, onion, salt-and-vinegar. She grabbed three small packs of the onion-flavored chips and took her things up to the front counter.

"They say it's clearing," the proprietor said, his face gray and squashed up a little. He placed her things in a white plastic bag. "But they've been wrong before."

An old woman in a blue raincoat mumbled something as Martha walked into the hotel. She picked up her key at the front desk and made her way across the lobby. The flat heels of her loafers, clack-clacking on the marble floor, made her suddenly self-conscious. A man was standing at the elevator, he seemed to be staring at her. It was too late to avoid him by going back to speak to the desk clerk. Too obvious. He'd sense her unease.

Thin and blond, with high cheekbones and a strong forehead, the man reminded her a little of a rock musician, someone she'd seen on an album cover, she couldn't remember his name, but she'd know his music. Terry had all his albums.

He'd pressed the button, the arrow in the brass plate was flashing red.

"I hope you're not in any hurry. This elevator's sleeping on the job," he said, scuffing the floor with the toe of his boot.

They both smiled because right then the doors opened. She got on first, her eye taking in the doodles and scratches on the grimy wall, discerning no meaning or pattern there. The man had long legs, the cuffs of his blue jeans were rolled up. They passed the third, the fourth, the fifth floor. The light would soon come on beside six, then seven, her floor.

"It's cleared up nicely," he said. "Should be able to see most of Rainier . . . . Mountains, they're something else, aren't they? Day like today they'll seem like they're sitting right in your backyard."

She let his words hang in the air.

"Can I ask you something . . . ?"

She'd be getting out soon, opening the door of her bright corner room. She saw herself standing at the window, looking across the bay.

"Would you like to come up to the roof with me, check out the view?"

"I'm sorry. I'm not sure I understand . . . ." The usual line was, 'Has anyone told you you really look like ____?' (in her case, it was often Catherine Deneuve).

"It's a terrific view. Honest. Besides Rainier, there's Mount Saint Helens and Baker to the north. I can point them out for you. The view's as good as you'll get in Seattle, except maybe from the Space Needle."

"Is there a restaurant up there?"

"No. There's not that. But the view . . . It's . . . It'll wow you."

"Thank you, but I don't think so." She stepped into the murky corridor.

"Why? Heights bother you?"

The elevator door was closing. He reached out and pushed it back with the palm of his hand.

"No. I'm not usually afraid of heights."

"So what's holding you back then?"

"I'm just not sure I'm up for it."

The door began to close again, doing what it was programmed to do. He tapped it with the side of his hand, causing it to change direction. "I guess this is why the elevator's so slow." They both laughed. "Honestly, the view's amazing. Aren't you curious? Don't you want to see it?"

"All right. All right. I'll come." She stepped back into the elevator. *Turn away from your fear and it grows.*

A girlfriend had once told her it was a good idea to let a man you were meeting for the first time think you had a boyfriend. But the way she felt now, she was beyond all that . . . the only thing now was to go with the flow. *Turn away from your fear and it grows.* It wouldn't matter what he had in mind, what he planned to hit her up with, what trip he might lay on her — though, in some other part of her mind, she sensed his banter was genuine, the view of mountains he was offering was real. So what if the guy was offering more than a view from the roof. So what if she learned some of the details of whatever he was locked into mortal combat with.

The elevator door wouldn't budge now. He pulled at the black rubber membrane inside the groove. Still it didn't release.

"Okay door, don't close, see if I care." He stood back and delivered a judo chop to the membrane.

The door fell into line, inching across the open space and closing.

They got out on the ninth floor and the next thing she knew she'd stepped through the sturdy brown metal door at the end of the corridor. She found herself on the landing of a fire escape, thin iron slats between her and the ground nine floors below. A rickety marine ladder led to the roof. Tiny fissures had sprouted in the bricks of the facade where the bolts securing the ladder had been hammered in.

"Hold tight to each rung and look up, look up to where you want to go. You don't want to look down."

She gripped the third rung from the bottom and pulled herself up, positioning her feet on the lowest rung. Fixing her eye on the hoop at the top of the ladder, she climbed, rung by rung, cool air from the bay lapping at her legs. At the top, she squeezed through the hoop and swung her body onto the pebblestone roof.

Sunlight flared down the sides of the nearby office buildings, panes of colored glass and the lacquered metals of the late twentieth century — chromium grays, slate blacks, phenolic reds. Through the open spaces between these sunswept buildings, she could see out across perhaps a hundred miles of valley.

"There's Rainier," he pointed to a purple luminescence on the horizon, barely visible below the halo of white cloud. "You can't see the others. I was here in June once and I saw them all clear as crystal. Adams and Rainier, and Hood tucked in between the two . . . . It's something, isn't it?" he said, walking away, leaving her alone to make what she would of the view.

For a while, she pondered the cone of molten rock and glacial ice in the distance, the mist shimmering and settling over the land, blurring the green valley. When she looked up to see where he'd gotten to, she saw no one. Then he appeared in a band of sunlight, standing thirty feet away, the toe of one boot extending over the edge. She inched over to what she guessed was the northwest corner of the building. Not much to see here, just a scrawl of gray roads and parking lots, cratered building sites, a yellowed-out horizon that reminded her of Kathmandu in summer.

On the Pacific side, blackened piers and the corrugated roofs of warehouses gave way to the sparkle of Elliott Bay. Looking south, the office buildings seemed to whirl in the sky, the air itself, ubiquitous and thin, yawning between them. There was no skin connecting the slick surfaces of things. Each structure was the product of its own gonadal force, its sole mission in life seemed to be that of competing with its neighbor. Nothing about these steel and glass towers gave much comfort to the soul. In the blink of an eye, it could all disappear and maybe it wouldn't matter.

A tower in the distance seemed to tilt in toward the one next to it. It took her a while to realize this was an optical effect, not the first stagger of apocalypse. Once the umbilical cord was cut at birth, all certainty ended and any shelter a human being might find was easily disrupted. Something sharp pierced the white of her eye. She rubbed at it, thinking about the lethal effect of one tiny fleck of dirt, then for some reason the crazy thought came to her that her own security depended on the technicians in the missile silos along the coast who were often blitzed out on junk food. She'd read about that in one of her mother's left-wing magazines.

She expected the panic to come, but it didn't. *Turn away from your fear and it grows.*

"It was worth it, huh?"

His voice startled her.

"The view's . . . . I can never find words for it," he was rubbing the back of his neck beneath his blond hair. "But I'll tell you this, the view's why I stay here. You may not care to believe me when I say this, but I don't have to stay in this old dump. I could be shacked up in a Holiday Inn or a Best Western, but I wouldn't be able to open the window if I did. Would I?"

"You probably wouldn't."

"Wouldn't be able to turn off the air conditioning either. Probably get that Legionnaire's Disease." His back was to the sun. "Can't stand air conditioning."

She squinted and looked down at the pebblestone roof, troubled by a tingling sensation in her legs.

"I like to breathe the air that's outside."

"I know what you mean."

"You hungry at all?"

"No. Not really."

"Why don't I buy us something to eat, or maybe a drink, a coffee or something? Pike Street Market's not far."

"I'm not sure I'm up for that right now."

"I could tell you about the mountains. Half a dozen people die every year trying to climb Rainier, did you know that?"

"Look. I'd like you to understand something. I'm in no mood. I'm just in no mood for what you're thinking."

"I'm not thinking anything."

They were quiet for a moment. He stood in the light that had spilled over the roof, face in shade, his fingers jammed into the pockets of his jeans. It seemed to her then that the raw energy in the world, its mutant force, its wildness, could be captured up here.

A roar came from somewhere to the south — an airplane moved across the crack of sky between two office towers, disappeared behind the darker tower, then reappeared again several seconds later, veering over the bay. He would want to tell the story of his life. Most men were impatient to tell you about all the horrible things that'd happened to them, as if fishing for sympathy were a turn-on for a woman.

"It's not that I don't want to join you for lunch," she paused, tracking the plane, now dipping into the haze over Sea-Tac Airport. "It's just that I've got a lot to do this afternoon."

"Well, then what possessed you to get up on this roof?" he joked, pushing his fingers through his long wavy hair. "I could be nutso. For all you know, I could be the Wild Man of Borneo."

• • •

He made his way down. It was best, he said, if he went first. She dropped to her knees and lay down on the roof, then rolled on her side and edged herself backward through the hoop onto the ladder, her knuckles whitening as she clasped the top rung. She stepped down, one foot at a time. It was fine until, confused by the irregular distance between the bottom rung and the landing, she let go too early, dropping awkwardly, going over on her ankle and lurching sideways, her hip crashing against the railing.

His arm shot out to catch her before she hurtled over. He steadied her, then, with his arm around her waist, gently piloted her through the thick door. Once safely inside the corridor, she went to thank him and found herself seeking out his mouth. He pulled her to him. The next thing she knew he was fumbling with a key, opening the door to a room, just down the corridor, then they were inside and she was slipping out of her jeans. It was fresh, a breeze off the bay chilling into the room from wide-open windows, but she didn't care.

A few hours later, he got up to close the windows. She took a good look at him, admiring his muscled shoulders and arms. While he was inside her, she'd run her hands down his sides and over his taut rump. Their lovemaking was overdriven. She wasn't really in any state of mind to think about how she might describe him while they were doing what they did, but if someone had asked her afterward, she would've had to say, corny as it sounded, the chemistry was good. She kept on wanting him even though his lovemaking was a little awkward. He hadn't let her pleasure him in the way she liked and he'd thrust in and out too vigorously. But he was big inside her, a throbbing kinesthetic presence. At one point, she'd nestled up to his ear, asked if this was what he'd had in mind when he'd waited for her at the elevator.

Some primordial voice had told her to make it with this man. That he could be the antidote for her dread. And so far it'd worked. She closed her eyes, letting her mind drift, vaguely aware of the afternoon passing, the sun moving lower in the sky, the room cooling down. At first, it was peaceful lying beside him in the dwindling light, listening to the gulls, the distant clang of machinery, a stentorian voice barking over a loudspeaker at one of the wharves. But at a certain point, after staring for a long time at the ceiling tiles, water-stained and punctured with thousands of identical holes, she found herself craving the pills in her room.

She slid quietly out of bed and located her clothes on a rickety chair. The only sound inside the room was the man's breathing. Chinese cooking seeped up from somewhere below, the smell of peanut oil chokingly fetid. He stirred in the bed. She pulled on her jeans. Out the window, she could see the red lights of a barge anchored in the bay.

"What's so interesting out there?"

"There's quite a wind over the bay."

He flicked on the bedside lamp. In the low light, his thin face looked haunted, as if he'd been under some strain, a prisoner of some inner compulsion. Or maybe it was just hard living.

"My name's Bob, by the way," he said, digging his elbows into the mattress, sitting up in the bed. "Truth is, though, it's just a nickname."

She could hear men laughing somewhere, wondered if they were the same men she'd heard lying in bed last night.

"My real name's something else . . . not sure I want to tell you what it is . . . ."

"Don't be coy. I'd like to know your real name."

"Okay, you asked for it. It's Gunnar . . . . For thirty-three years, I was ashamed of that name. Now I no longer am. But I got called Bob for so many years I . . . well, I sometimes still think of myself as Bob Olson."

"Gunnar's a nicer name than Bob."

Consequences would attach to what they were now saying. There was still a bond between them, carnal and unspoken. The danger was that, as the bond dissolved, as the differences between them became apparent, he'd feel ashamed of his own desire and turn nasty. Some men were like that.

He did physical labor, she knew that much. His arms and neck were a shade darker than his shoulders and chest. He was hard to read, the tough-guy veneer was forced. He wasn't a grifter with some mean agenda up his sleeve. She was sure of that. And if he had another side, a crazy side, she hadn't seen it yet.

She vowed to tell him the minimum — that she lived in Vancouver, was on her way to visit her mother in a hospital in Portland. In her experience, it was best to say as little as possible to a stranger. That way, he was more likely to think of you in the way he wanted, and the unspoken bond could be preserved for as long as possible.

"These days I'm a waitress," she said when he asked what she did in Vancouver. "But I'd rather not talk about it."

"That's cool," he said. "Want to know what I do for a living?"

It wouldn't matter how she answered, she thought to herself, he'd tell her anyway. She came and sat on the bed, relieved to be off the hook. For now anyway.

"Most chicks want to know what a guy does, don't they?"

"I guess they do."

"I'm in the forestry business."

She wrapped her arms around her chest to keep warm.

"I bet you're thinking 'Oh, no, a redneck!'"

"What?"

"People like you think all loggers are rednecks, isn't that so?"

"People like me?"

"You know, if I was a logger, I wouldn't hide that fact. Loggers are good people. I've worked with them. I used to be a reforestation engineer," he crossed his arms behind his head. "I even have a business card which'll attest to that."

She understood then that he wasn't a Don Juan, he was looking for more than a fling, he was putting some cards on the table to make himself post-coitally memorable. He was in town for an interview, a forestry job, he lived in a place called Longview, was driving back there the next day. It wasn't far from Portland.

When he grew silent, she got up from the bed and went into the bathroom. The mirror over the cracked sink had oxidized, turning her head into an amorphous blur. She splashed cold water on her face, let the water tingle her pores, then patted her cheeks dry with her hands.

"Do you have a boyfriend?" he shouted from the next room.

"No."

"Ever been married?"

"No."

"Ever come close?"

"No."

"I'd marry you."

"You would?"

"Yeah. You've got a nice body."

She put her mouth under the tap, careful not to touch it, and took several gulps. If only she were here with Terry. He didn't need the constant attention, the craving for sympathy most heterosexual men seemed to need. She switched off the light over the sink.

"I have to go."

He beckoned for her to come back and sit on the bed.

She shook her head.

He got out of bed, came over to where she was standing and hugged her. "You know what we just did, I'd like to do it again."

"I really do have to go." She looked down at the worn linoleum floor.

"Okay."

She ran her fingers through his hair.

He hugged tighter.

She felt him getting hard and stepped away, not wanting it to go further, too sore to start in again with him.

"Was the view of the mountains worth it?"

"Yes. It was."

• • •

Two floors below, Martha munched on onion-flavored potato chips and sipped warm apple juice from a carton. What she'd done with the man didn't shock her particularly. She'd staved off a panic attack. *Turn away from your fear and it grows.* Her desire was good, nothing to be frightened of. She'd enjoyed his lean body. And that was okay in her mind. The plan was to meet in the lobby at nine in the morning. He wasn't going that far, but he'd drive her to Portland anyway. Meeting downstairs was the best arrangement. One of them could always chicken out, she thought to herself as she slipped an Ativan under her tongue.

THE ROAD

The morning was windless, typical of November in the Northwest, foggy of course. You could barely make out the low-rise buildings on the far side of the parking lot.

He slammed down the hood and got into the car beside her.

"Not bad, huh?"

Martha looked at him blankly.

"My machine. It's not an old heap."

He was referring to his car, it was souped up, the kind of car you'd be sure to notice on the road, a gold hatchback with fat racing tires. The rear seat had been folded down into a platform that was cluttered with bags of what looked like dirty laundry, a sleeping roll and ground sheet, a glacier-blue Nalgene water bottle, several fishing rods, and other gear she didn't know the use of.

"There's ten feet of sleeping room back there," he said, turning the key in the ignition. "But I'm not as young as I used to be. Can't sleep in a car no more. There's actually a lot of things I don't do any more. Some things I still like doing though, like last night."

She said nothing, sex didn't have to be sacred, but it wasn't something you wanted to be coy about.

He revved the motor. "Do you know what kind of car this is?"

"A Corvette?"

"This here's a Plymouth Barracuda. Not many of these cars still on the road."

They followed the signs for the entrance to the interstate, passing a bunch of used-car dealerships, colorful pennants strung around the rain-soaked asphalt parking lots. She looked over at him. The long hair worked because of his high cheekbones and strong nose. He was good-looking, she saw that now.

"This is the best car General Motors ever made. Don't ask me why they stopped making it."

On the interstate, cracked concrete walls and the water-stained abutments of bridges hulked in around them. The traffic had slowed to a crawl because of the fog.

"They say this is the most liveable city in the country," he shouted over the din of a truck's motor. "I don't get it. There's no street life any more. Downtown's no longer a place people come to after dark. Everything's happening at the malls now."

She wouldn't have noticed Boeing Field had he not pointed it out, a string of gray hangars cloaked in fog, two parallel lines of hazy orange lights illuminating what was perhaps a test runway.

"You know something," he said. "You're a super lady."

"Let's not spoil this."

"Spoil what? I'm complimenting you. There are some real bimbos out there."

Martha pictured him at a bar with a trashy blonde in a short leather skirt and cowboy boots. But she also saw that he was troubled by his own imperfect grasp of who he was, and this recognition drew her a little closer to him.

By the time they got to Tacoma, the wind had picked up and the fog was lifting.

"My mom lives in Tacoma. She thinks I only visit her when I'm broke. I don't know how she can say that. Last week I took her to a seafood restaurant in Forrester's Mall. We had a great meal . . . ." He stopped speaking, Martha hearing dismay and perhaps despair in the whishing of his exhaled breath. "There's times, though, I am broke. She fixes steak and we sit and watch *Wide World of Sports*."

Martha knew men liked to watch sports on television, but Gunnar was the first man she'd met who admitted it.

"My parents went their separate ways when I was six. My father, he spent pretty much his whole life on oil rigs, had to have one of his feet amputated several years back. He's down in Baton Rouge now, with a woman from the Philippines."

Martha was happy to let him talk. He was probably lonely, used to spending weekends watching TV in some poorly ventilated room. Some people just needed to get things off their chest.

"My brother, he didn't react too well to the divorce. He was way too wild for mom to look after. She had to put him in foster care. He just seemed to invite trouble after that, it was like he needed to piss people off. He ended up in the reformatory at Chehalis."

Martha looked up, the sky to the south was clearing. Though she found his brawny voice comforting, she told herself she'd have to be careful. She didn't want him saying something he'd later regret.

"I hoped he might've outgrown his moodiness in the army, but six months after getting back from Vietnam, he goes and picks up this hitchhiker, a psychology student at the University of Puget Sound. The young woman was a nutcase, she accused him of raping her."

She leaned back in the seat, arms crossed and cradled for warmth, elbows resting in her opened palms.

He stared ahead at the road, not seeking her eyes, she liked that, much easier to be with someone who doesn't need your approval.

"The evidence pointed to her having consented to sex, but the judge, knowing there's a criminal record, refuses to plea bargain it down, the bastard makes sure my brother goes to Walla Walla, says he needs to protect society from rapists."

Sunlight swept across the land, then dimmed just as suddenly, the sun passing behind an armada of fast-moving clouds.

"Everything is emotional," Gunnar said. "It's important to do what feels right, but what feels right to you sometimes doesn't sit right with other people."

Some time after Tacoma, they left the interstate and headed for the coast. She began to feel pleasantly drowsy, welcoming sleep, having slept fitfully that night, waking several times to use the toilet, getting spooked by a crying baby, unsure if the cries were in her dream, or coming up from the room below through the water pipes.

Somewhere along the way, they stopped at a Food Ranch. She got a coffee in a plastic cup, he picked up a six-pack and a handful of grain-based snacks.

"I like to be fit," he said. "It's hard to drink beer and stay fit. I keep my weight down by eating lots of cereal."

Nearing the coast, they drove through big timber country, coming upon places where the forest had been clear-cut.

"I met an environmentalist once," he said. "A lady from California. Millions in the bank, but she didn't know the first thing about trees, didn't know the difference between balsam and cedar."

"You're not an environmentalist, then," she said tentatively. She'd torn a little strip off her coffee lid but the coffee, still hot, scalded her tongue.

"No sirree. No ma'am. I'm not," he paused. "Actually I agree with a lot of what they say. Trees aren't wheat. That's true. Depending on your type of tree, it takes anywhere from forty to a hundred and twenty years for a second-growth forest to come back."

He drove with one hand, held his can of beer in the other.

"Trees aren't wheat," he repeated, using the beer can to rub the back of his neck under his long hair, "but timber is definitely a crop. You can't quarrel with the lumber industry's methods. An environmentalist will tell you that unless one tree is planted for every one that's cut down, the forest will disappear. That's bullshit."

Martha hated that word, hated the kind of people, men mostly, who sprinkled it into their conversations. Her mother used the word a lot. *Liberal bullshit.* That was one of her mother's favorite expressions.

"It'll never happen. For one simple reason. Forests naturally reseed themselves."

Martha sipped the coffee. People had their own strong opinions, their own certainties. She felt the lack of that. She could usually see both sides of an issue. It came from having parents who'd divorced.

"A lot of reseeding nowadays is done by planes. No one wants to see the forests disappear. Are you kidding? You don't see logging operators going in and clear-cutting the way they used to. They cut with a view to replanting. Which means paying attention to soil conditions. Operators nowadays will leave some trees standing in order to kickstart the reseeding cycle."

He pointed to a stand of scraggly trees at the edge of the forest. "You see those trees? Do you know what they are?"

"Poplar?"

"Close. Aspen. Those trees are just like weeds. They'll grow back in a decade and grow back healthier."

One summer in junior high, Martha had joined an all-girl tree-planting expedition. Their brigade, she recalled, was asked to do ten acres on the fringe of the Tillamook Forest, the country around Hell's Canyon. They'd planted from dawn to noon and from three to six, resting during the heat of the afternoon, lying around in their tents talking about the boys they had crushes on. For lunch they ate peanut-butter-and-jelly sandwiches, washing them down with sodas. In the evening they roasted salmon trout and sat around the campfire listening to Indian legends. On Saturday afternoons, if they were good, they'd be driven in to the dairy in Gales Creek and treated to fudgsicles.

"My grandmother worked in a cannery for twenty-nine years," Gunnar said. "Not far from here. Hard to believe a person could work in a fish factory that long and be happy, but she was."

They were entering the town of Raymond now, turning onto a side road of sprawling factories that manufactured glues, plastics, polyester fibers and strange substances she'd never heard of. It was an ugly view, a progression of windowless gray buildings, some with tall smokestacks, most with huge parking lots enclosed by chain-link fencing. He turned into one of the lots, driving past an unattended security booth. A billboard boasted that this particular plant was the world's leading manufacturer of cellulose acetate flake for cigarette filters.

"You see that flag? You probably think a woman named Betsy Ross designed it," he said, pointing to the enormous Stars and Stripes that flew on a flagpole out front. "If you're like me, you learned that in the first grade. Well, it's just a myth. I found that out watching a game show."

He pulled into the row of cars farthest from the building, next to a blue spruce hedge that concealed a line of rusty gasoline drums.

"I guess you want to know what we're doing here," he said, opening his throat, gulping the rest of his beer, then crushing the can. "I worked in this hellhole for a couple of months during the summer. They owe me some severance."

He affected a limp as he crossed the asphalt parking lot.

She waited until he'd disappeared into the building before opening the glove compartment. Magazines and a little red-and-yellow can came crashing down onto her feet. She picked up the can. DRI & GO. Something you sprayed on the ignition wires and distributor cap to get rid of moisture. The instructions said to spray liberally. She shoved the can back into the glove compartment, then picked up the magazines, wildlife magazines mostly, plus a soft-covered manual, *Small Gas Engines, Fundamentals, Service and Troubleshooting Repairs* by

Alfred C. Roth, Assistant Professor of Industrial Education, Eastern Michigan State University, Ypsilanti. She studied the box-and-arrow diagrams that showed how chainsaws and lawn mowers worked. The manual made her think of *Zen and the Art of Motorcycle Maintenance*, one of those books she'd begun but never finished.

He was back in less than five minutes, muttering under his breath as he yanked the car door open. "No luck," he said. "They think I'm just a grunt, that I won't follow this up with a lawyer. They don't know me."

• • •

Fifteen minutes later, they were at a waterfront restaurant in South Bend, seated in a cherry-red vinyl booth, wind from the ocean rattling the windows. The back door of the restaurant was open, letting in light from the cluttered yard behind. The place had a soggy, salty smell. Carved wooden ducks and a plastic yellow bird, a *Sesame Street* character, gathered dust on the shelf above the bar.

A waitress with a deep tan brought them menus, automatically turning over her coffee cup and filling it. Gunnar, putting his hand over his cup, asked for a Coors.

"You have beautiful eyes," he said after the waitress had gone. "I could fall for you."

"You don't know anything about me."

"I know what I know."

She felt him studying her. There was a hairline crack in the lip of her coffee cup.

"I don't do this every day," he began. "I don't ever like to pester people. Live and let live, that's my motto."

"I like the motto."

"Can I be frank with you?"

"Of course."

"Well, there's one thing I'd like to straighten out."

She watched the waitress rub lotion onto her brown arms.

"I happen to think honesty is important, and I lied to you about something."

She was waiting for him to say he was married, but that wasn't it.

"My brother isn't doing time at Walla Walla . . . I don't have a brother."

"What?"

"It was me who picked up that woman."

"What woman?"

"The psychology student."

Sun glinted on a sheet of aluminum out in the backyard.

"I'm not telling you this because I feel bad. No way. I did what I did. I'm not ashamed to admit it. I paid for it too. Nine years of my life. I did five-and-a-half years in Walla Walla, then almost three years in the Willipa Hills, clearing deadfall, keeping Washington green."

He began rubbing the soft skin below his eye with his index finger. He was working something through, he'd been wounded by things that had happened in his past. They had that in common.

"I don't rightly know why I'm telling you this."

"I'm not finding it weird, if that's what you're worried about."

"Can I tell you something?"

She nodded, liking his face, the way pain was worn into it.

"You're the first woman I've talked to for more than three seconds in a long, long time. I haven't had what you'd call a normal life for nineteen years. Can you remember where you were nineteen years ago?"

"I'd have to think about it."

"Nineteen years ago, I was a different person . . . ."

A song came on the radio, she remembered listening to it on a trip she'd taken with her parents when she was just a kid, maybe eight or nine years old.

> Her tender lips are sweeter than honey
> And Wolverton Mountain protects her there
> The bears and the birds
> Tell Clifton Clowers if a stranger should enter there.

"As far as the rape goes," he resumed. "There were extenuating circumstances. What I did wasn't particularly delicate, but it wasn't rape, not to my way of thinking. I didn't force her to do anything she didn't want to, but the cops decided to make the charge stick, since I'd already done a stretch at Chehalis when I was seventeen. Not for rape, I should add. For robbing a dry cleaner's. Smart, huh? For that little caper, I got a coat that didn't fit and eighteen months in reformatory."

"You really don't have to be telling me this," she said, though she wanted him to go on. He was inviting her into his world, making her feel less alone in hers. A kinship was forming between them. Maybe she could help him redeem himself, help him take back a little of what the world had taken from him.

"I know that, and I know I'm not exactly putting you at ease. But think about it. If I were a rapist, would I be telling you this?"

The waitress came over and asked if everything was okay. Martha had buried most of her gristly cutlet underneath some mashed potatoes. Gunnar, who'd taken only a few bites of his sausage, waved her away.

"You don't want to hear the story of my life. So I'll put it all in a nutshell for you. I made one mistake, one dumb little mistake. I acted stupid for five minutes. You don't know how many times I've prayed to God asking to have those five minutes to do over again."

The waitress was staring at him. She'd overheard him say he was a rapist, was that it? Or was it his wavy blond hair, his rock-star good looks?

"I was a different person then. I got back from Vietnam in July of '69, the week of the moon walk. I remember standing around on the main street of Raymond. A few days earlier I'd been in the jungle, retreating from enemy machine-gun fire, not thinking about anything except who was on both sides of me. Death wasn't something I worried about. When you're dead, so far as I know, you're not aware of being dead. Isn't that so?"

> *Her tender lips are sweeter than honey*
> *and Wolverton Mountain protects her there.*

"I'd just been through hell and no one cared. I didn't really have any friends. People were glad to see me, glad I was alive. But they had no idea what I'd been through. They expected me to be the same. But I wasn't the same. I was a nervous wreck. I felt somebody owed me something. Besides, I didn't want to hang around and drink myself into an early grave. I just couldn't see going back to the cannery. So I moved up to Tacoma, started working odd jobs . . ."

I don't care about Clifton Clowers
I'm gonna climb up on his mountain
I'm gonna take the girl I love.

". . . got to drinking too much, started hanging out at the sports bars on the Sea-Tac strip where the live entertainment used to be Go-Go dancers, still is, I guess. I'd be tempted to go home with one of them, but I knew I'd probably feel lousy after . . ."

The bears and the birds
Tell Clifton Clowers if a stranger should enter there.

". . . sure I checked out the dating bars, chicks there, you know, they're looking for men in three-piece suits. I got pretty desperate so I began cruising, driving around pretty near all night. I got used to it. It became the natural thing. You know what I'm saying?"

His fists were tightly clenched, he was staring at a place behind her head.

"Well, I didn't think there was anything wrong with me. Maybe I was a little down. I was staying out of trouble, though. I'd been working as a roofer for six months when it happened . . . . You know what the judge said when he sentenced me, the bastard said that as far as he could tell, I did it for kicks. That's why a long sentence was in order. Twelve years. And I did nine."

• • •

She held his hand as they strolled along the boardwalk, surf pounding the rocks, sending spray up over the road in places. No one looking at them would have guessed they'd just met.

"You know, I didn't have to say anything. I leveled with you, though, because I don't want there to be any dishonesty between us."

A flock of geese flew low over marshland in the distance. Two women wearing sun visors jogged toward them, their ponytails wagging from side to side behind their heads. Gunnar turned around to check out the backs of their tanned legs.

"Do you jog?"

"I'm a waitress, remember, I don't need the exercise."

They stopped to watch some pelicans dive-bomb the water, the sky above sweetening to blue in places. He put his arm around her shoulders, kissed the back of her neck. She pulled away gently.

In a touristy store that sold shells, Indian wood carvings and necklaces of brightly colored stones, Martha bought a scented candle for her mother. From a pay telephone outside, she dialed the number she had for the hospital. The phone rang a while before an irritated male voice picked up.

"Yeah. Emerg."

"Is Mrs. Spencer there?"

"She could be here for all I know. What's her problem?"

"Oh, uh, I'm not sure . . . I'd like to come for a visit, I just wanted to be sure, you know, that it'd be okay . . . ."

"Listen. Why you botherin' us? Call patient inquiry," the voice snapped and was gone.

"Fucking ridiculous," Martha muttered into the phone before hanging up.

• • •

They followed the coast down to the Columbia, the ridges of pine forest getting lost in billowing white cloud. At the mouth of the river, they took the north shore, driving up into the mountains.

"You wouldn't believe what it was like at that camp," Gunnar said. "I felt like I was a hundred years old, spending all that time with kids. Bad apples too. A couple of them made my life miserable, keeping me awake with their heavy-metal music."

The barren peak of Mount Saint Helens came into view, miles to the north. The road here seemed to run right into the clouds, the coast vanishing in mist farther and farther behind them. To the south it was as if pink paint, in bright thin arcs and thicker curls, had been sprayed over a dimming white canvas. It would be perfect, she thought to herself, if this drive never ended.

"They used to truck us all over Washington State," he continued, a large vein pulsing in his neck. "It was mostly ditchdiggers' work. They pushed us pretty hard. I fell out of a tree the first week I was there, got a concussion. That's when the brain is literally shaken around inside the skull and the tissues are bruised. My memory went plum dead. I didn't know my name or anything. All I knew was that I was a human being and that a human being was something complicated to be. I knew I had a problem, not knowing who I was. The more uptight I got, the harder it was for me to remember. Fortunately, after a few days, it all came back to me."

Every now and then, Mack trucks hurtled toward them, careening around the sharp turns, the drivers high up in the red cabs, their faces a blur. The road narrowed as they went farther into the forest, the big rigs taking on a life of their own, windshield wipers going because of the mist, blinking like eyelids, the chrome grills grinning like monsters from the deep.

"It was a nightmare. If it weren't for the kids, though, I could've enjoyed myself. I didn't mind the work, except for picking pinecones. That got monotonous. We used hair dryers to dry off the sticky sap, then we shipped them out to pharmaceutical company labs all over the country."

They'd been on the road an hour when they passed through the hamlet of Grays River. The sun was well over the Pacific but still high enough in the sky to cast some of its rays over the shingled roofs of half a dozen weathered wood houses. In a meadow on the outskirts, a ramshackle log cottage, a sloppily painted sign out front, 'Dun Workin' Manor.'

"There wasn't anything to do at night," he continued, rubbing the bridge of his nose with his index finger, "except play cards and read science fiction. I pretty near went out of my mind."

Her duffel bag was in the back. She could easily reach it, find her cosmetics case, rummage through it for a white angel, wash it down with a swig of beer. But she didn't feel the need of Valium. Being with this guy was answering something in her she'd forgotten existed.

"I know I'm gabbing about it now, but I don't dwell on all the years I lost. What would be the point? You may find this strange, but I learned a lot there. Prison changed me. Hell, it changes everybody.

Usually for the worse. In one way, though, it changed me for the better. I don't think I'd be as happy doing what I'm doing if I hadn't gone. I'd probably want more of what money can buy, a big house, a better car than this old heap, stereo speakers . . . I wouldn't mind stereo speakers." He laughed. "I guess if I hadn't done time, I'd have ambitions to be a businessman, sit in a swivel chair and take responsibility for what happens."

There were still wisps of pink cloud in the sky, the shimmering peak of Mount Saint Helens looming in and out of view on the left as they rounded the curves. Up here, there was no place for deceit or human pretension. At some point after Skamokawa, they came upon an elk herd gathered in a clearing. He pulled over and backed the car down the grassy side of the road so they could watch the animals munch whatever it was the ranger was shoveling out from the back of his tractor. She rolled down the window, letting in the fresh air. The animals stood motionless, antlers catching the light, eyes gleaming. The land rose sharply beyond the clearing, log steps cut into the side of the hill leading up to a weathered hut. Several of the herd shook their shaggy tufted manes and made for the higher ground, moving in unison past the hut and disappearing in the woods.

Martha remembered something Gunnar had said earlier. *Everything is emotional.* He was right about that.

"You know something, Gunnar," she said, thinking of her mother in the hospital. "Human beings are quite ignorant. Human beings don't know the first thing about life."

Gunnar fixed his eyes straight ahead. With daylight relinquishing its hold on the road, they drove in silence, crossing the Columbia and turning south toward Portland.

MULTNOMAH
COUNTY HOSPITAL

Her mother lay on her back, matted strands of gray hair falling over her cheek, her face swollen and disfigured by raised crimson plaques. A tube entered her chest just below the collarbone, it was held in place by a bloodied bandage and surgical tape. Two bags of clear fluid, one labeled Dextrose, the other, Potassium Chloride, dangled on the IV pole next to the bed.

Martha kissed her mother lightly on the forehead, then went over to the window. She could see Portland in the distance, the Union Station clock tower encased in rusty scaffolding. Though the hands and several of the Roman numerals had fallen off, the clock's creamy white face was still intact. Beyond the tower lay West Hills, a rorschach of flickering yellow light. One of those winking lights was the ceramic-tiled kitchen in the house her father shared with Jean Fogarty. Another was the rosewood sunroom on the second floor, Martha thinking, they were so materialistic, their house was right out of *Architectural Digest*.

She stood there a while, listening to her mother's labored breathing, afraid she might suddenly wake up, thinking that this was how they'd always got along, ships passing in the night.

She tiptoed out of the room, glimpsing a white-clad figure darting behind the glass-partitioned nursing station at the end of the corridor.

"Excuse me," Martha said, addressing two nurses who were conferring in front of a pink chalkboard. "Can you tell me how Mrs. Spencer's doing? I'm her daughter."

"I'm not really in a position to tell you much, but I can try," one of them said, going over and grabbing a thick orange binder from the metal shelf on the wall. The name tag pinned to her collar said Dawne. "Your mother came in screaming, she kept the floor awake the first night she was here. Then something went wrong. Possibly a stroke. She's been a lot quieter since then, still nervous though, whimpers a lot, cries out at night, occasionally talks to herself . . . ."

"A stroke. What does that mean? Is she able to . . . to, you know, talk . . . or, I mean, to walk."

"Not really. But I wouldn't worry. It's early days. Her lack of mobility is probably temporary. We see it all the time on this floor." The nurse frowned as she flipped through the pages of the binder. "Oh, I see. It says here your mother may have had a brain seizure, she's finding it difficult to move her legs."

Spencer was printed on the binder in black letters. Her mother had kept her father's name.

"By the way, we've been giving her Demerol. Is that okay with you?"

"Uh, I guess so . . . . What does Demerol do?"

"It's a narcotic, makes her easier to manage. We prefer it. But if for any reason you want her lucid at the end, we won't give it to her."

"I don't know . . . I guess it's okay."

"The resident who ordered it should be on the floor later. Maybe he'll have some answers for you."

As Martha turned to go, the nurse sighed to herself. "We do our best," she said, "there are no miracles in medicine."

• • •

Martha sat at the foot of the bed, staring at the metal water pitcher glimmering like a bad dream on the windowsill, thinking this was serious, this might be it. The night table was cluttered with a jar of Vaseline, the novel *Shogun* in paperback, a yellowed copy of *Willamette Week*, and several magazines. Her mother was an avid magazine reader — for years, she'd subscribed to *Mother Jones*, as well as something called *The Insurgent Sociologist* published down in Eugene.

There was a cork bulletin board on the wall beside the bed, nothing much on it, no Get Well cards or snapshots of family and friends. Her mother hadn't had any visitors, at least not according to the nurse. Yet there'd been a time, during the Laurelhurst years, when the phone never stopped ringing.

One item on the bulletin board was hard to ignore, a pen-and-ink sketch of a bearded Jesus, his cross floating in a stormy sky. Below the garish picture, a short prayer in gothic lettering.

MOST SWEET JESUS

I welcome You, Most Sweet Jesus, into my room in order that You may ease my troubled mind.

I welcome You, Most Sweet Jesus, into my heart in order that You may console me in my sorrow and give me strength.

I welcome You, Most Sweet Jesus, into my room in order that You may deliver me from evil and bless my body.

I welcome You, Most Sweet Jesus, into my heart and know You will remain with me always.

I place my trust in You, Most Sweet Jesus.

Amen.

T. McCarthy, Office of the Chaplain, Multnomah County Hospital.

The rinpoche on Hornby Island had contended that Christians are at a loss when they come to experience the abyss. Buddhists take the abyss as their point of departure, he used to say. Her mother would scoff at that, not that her opinions were particularly relevant now. It hardly mattered that she'd once wanted to blow up the ROTC building at Portland State, or that just last year, she'd published a letter about the neutron bomb in *The Oregonian*.

It was the end of an era. Her mother was a Portland Johnson, the daughter of Maude Witter Johnson. She'd come out as a debutante in June of 1938, somewhere there existed an album of glossy photographs showing Clara Johnson dancing in the moonlit courtyard of the Normandy Hotel. That September, though, her mother had changed course, leaving for the University of Chicago, where she spent two years studying sociology, during which time she'd also joined the Communist League. Being a Communist wasn't so strange back then, her mother liked to say, since no one believed the economy would turn around without radical change in the structure of society.

In 1938 anyone with half a brain felt it necessary to fight "the mon-eyed interests." Her mother had been generous with her money, pro-vided the object of her charity was strangers. Martha had had to beg for five hundred dollars for an airplane ticket to get home from Kath-mandu. *Travel for its own sake is a bourgeois vice.* Yet her mother had felt no guilt about staying in expensive hotels during those so-called learn-ing sojourns in Paris, Berlin, Barcelona, and Rome. Over the years, she'd eaten through much of her wealth. When the remaining proper-ties on Northwest Johnson were sold, her accountant had advised her to avoid the capital gains tax by purchasing an annuity that would pro-vide her with an income for as long as she lived. But inflation had eaten into its purchasing power, and now there were medical bills that neces-sitated selling off the fixed income securities in the Johnson estate.

The room burst into light, an orderly appeared at the door and pushed in toward Martha with a gurney, bumping it against the wall.

"Oh, hello," he said, seeing Martha. "Mrs. Spencer's wanted in X-ray."

"She's sleeping," Martha whispered as she stood up.

The orderly shot her a thin-lipped smile. A wiry unshaven man in unpressed white ducks and a grimy hospital tunic. He shoved the bed over toward the window to make way for the gurney.

"Oh no. Not again. You see that?" He pointed to the bag on the floor, ballooning with yellow liquid. "Nurses," he jabbed at the call button beside her mother's head, "they just aren't very curious, not too curious at all."

"What's the trouble?" a voice crackled over the intercom.

"It's Lenny. Will you please send someone to 647."

"Inez'll be there as soon as she can."

"I still got a stack of requisitions for X-ray. Let's get someone on this. Sometime this century."

He turned to Martha. "I'd do it myself, but they need to keep a record. That bag's backing up on her . . . . I'll be back."

He left shaking his head, Martha taking note for the first time of the urine-filled tube twisting around the metal rungs at the side of the bed.

The orderly came back twenty minutes later, accompanied by a Mexican nurse, large white teeth in a bovine face, cold fury in her eyes. Her name tag said Inez.

"Have to check her vitals." The nurse pulled the cord at the side of the bed, the headboard light flickered on.

Her mother twitched in the bright fluorescent light. "Help," she moaned in a feeble voice Martha had never heard before.

"Yes, yes, Mrs. Spencer," the nurse spoke with a lisp. "We can't help you unless you keep still."

The nurse propped her mother's head on a pillow, slipped an electronic thermometer into her mouth, then took her pulse.

"Hundred one," the nurse mumbled to herself, jotting down the result on a small piece of paper.

"That means she has a fever, doesn't it?"

The nurse gave Martha a perfunctory nod.

"Why would she have a fever?"

"Maybe infection," the nurse said, taking her mother's blood pressure.

"An infection? What kind of infection?"

The nurse shrugged.

"I talked to Dawne a few minutes ago, she says my mother was screaming the other night. Is that because she's in a lot of pain?"

The nurse muttered to herself in Spanish before switching into English. "After midnight I'm off this floor," she said. "I don't know what happens. If your mother screams, I don't hear it."

Martha glared at the nurse, then looked away, realizing that the woman was obtuse, impervious to the feelings of others. She watched, her bewilderment growing, as the nurse pulled the empty bags from the IV pole, flung them still dripping with clear fluid into the waste basket in the corner, grabbed new bags off her cart, crinkling them as she read the labels, clumsily ripping them open and setting them up on the pole. Next, she attacked the catheter bag, angrily yanking at the plug, catching the sploosh of urine in a plastic bucket, carrying it to the bathroom, emptying it into the toilet.

"She's all yours now, Lenny."

Her mother's eyes widened as she was lifted onto the gurney, but she gave no sign of recognition. Her gown was torn, sagging folds of skin where her breasts used to be, and there were sores over her back and legs, even on her arms.

They took the service elevator to the basement where patients were lined up, some on gurneys, others in wheelchairs, all waiting to be escorted back up to their rooms.

"About time," a bearded technician said when they got to the X-ray lab. "I should've been out of here twenty minutes ago."

Martha watched them lift her mother off the gurney and deposit her on the metal table.

"Can I help?"

"No," the technician growled. "You'll have to wait outside."

Her mother's gown had been pulled up, her thighs and buttocks touching the cold plate.

"Do you have to be so rough?"

"Miss, everyone in here's sick. I treat everone exactly the same."

"Don't mind him," the orderly said after the technician had closed the door in their faces. "His day will come."

• • •

Martha made her way over to an unoccupied cluster of pink plastic chairs set around a formica-topped coffee table, also pink. She picked up a tabloid newspaper, read the headline. *Butch Goring's Gamble.* It was a story about ice hockey.

Her mother loved newspapers, she'd once had a byline for a radical paper. There'd been a brief period in the early seventies when she'd gotten her act together and started to write a book about the civil rights movement. She'd done quite a bit of research on it, even received an encouraging letter from a man named Earl somebody or other, who'd written a book on the Scottsboro boys. Although her mother could talk for hours about what she called the "southern injustice system," she was able to produce only the roughest draft of several chapters and the hostile reaction she got from the publishing companies sapped her will. She used to say that you had to be a Harvard professor to write about class injustice in America. If only she'd finished that first book, she might've had ambitions to write more.

An hour, perhaps longer, must have gone by when Martha felt someone staring at her. It was the orderly from before, his pencil-thin eyebrows knitted in uncertainty.

"Hasn't she gone back up yet?" he asked, beckoning her to follow him along the corridor.

It was quieter now, the patients lined up earlier had all been moved upstairs.

The orderly pushed open the door to the X-ray lab. There was her mother, half-uncovered on the table, light glaring off the cold polished metal.

"I'm truly sorry, miss," he said. "He was in a hurry to get home, the bastard, didn't bother calling to let us know. Slipped away through that door. It's a restricted area for the technicians back there. They come and go as they please."

• • •

Back upstairs, Martha resumed her vigil. It came to her then that people died in these rooms. *Turn away from your fear and it grows.* She began looking for a pattern in the dents and scrapes on the walls, trying to reassure herself there was some order in the world. In the next room, a man was calling out for a doctor.

If her mother were to awaken, Martha had no idea what she'd say. No idea even what to call her mother. She hadn't used 'Mom' since she was a teenager, but 'Clara' had never felt right either. It was her father who'd started referring to her mother as Clara. Clara was the crazy woman he'd married, and Martha was Clara's unhappy daughter.

Beginning to feel the onset of a hunger headache, Martha pictured the packages of chips and pretzels on the display rack in the grocery store in Seattle. Was that just yesterday? . . . God, she'd momentarily forgotten he was down there in the parking lot waiting. Too much was happening, too fast for her heart to absorb. He might've split by now for all she knew. He'd been a comfort in the car, but you had to be realistic, with most men, you could never afford to let your guard down. Sure, he'd said he'd wait, but, by now, he could be at a bar somewhere, maybe at one of the strip joints on North Williams. It was just a one-night stand, that was all it was, they'd met in an elevator. She could hear Terry talking to one of his gay friends, "An elevator. I mean, come on now!" Yes, you probably were deluded if you thought picking up a guy in an elevator could ever turn into something special. But the drive through the mountains that afternoon had been so magical, it affirmed something more than sex, the affairs she'd had in Boulder were mostly about sex. This seemed different.

There was a soft knock at the door. A small bearded man padded into the room. Very young, younger than she was.

"Excuse me. I'm Dr. Starr," he said, going over to her mother, placing a sallow hand on her forehead. "I've been reading your mother's file. You might be able to help us. Do you mind if I ask you a few questions?"

Martha sat forward on the edge of the chair.

"Any idea what drugs your mother's been taking during the last year?"

Her mother kept a stash of pills in her dresser drawer, anti-inflammatory drugs for her lupus, minor tranqs to get to sleep, analgesics for pain. Her mother made herself some pretty heavy-duty pain cocktails.

"I don't know all the names . . . I think she takes painkillers, Percocets, Percodan."

"Not a good idea. They're both potent narcotics, extremely addictive." He smiled wanly. "Too bad she doesn't have a drug plan. Then we'd have a proper record . . . we're trying out a number of things, corticosteroids to counteract the inflammation, they're making her slightly psychotic, Indocid to decrease the swelling in her joints, with Indocid, we need to be sure there's no bleeding in her bowel. She's getting both Dilaudid and Haloperidol. Dilaudid's an effective painkiller, Haloperidol's an antipsychotic, it increases the efficiency of the painkiller . . . and there's an order for Demerol at the discretion of the doctor on call, tonight that's me."

"She doesn't recognize me."

"I know. We think she might've had a petit mal seizure."

"A what?"

"A petit mal seizure. A kind of epileptic attack that can be brought on by alcohol."

"Oh. I see."

"Do you know if she's ever taken a drug called Dilantin?"

"I have no idea."

"Has she ever had psychiatric treatment?"

"She's seen psychiatrists."

"By psychiatric treatment, I mean specifically electroshock."

"I don't think so, but I can't say for sure."

"The X-rays suggest altered density in the cerebellum. We think something is attacking her brain. Do you know if she has a history of blackouts?"

"I don't think so, she likes to drink."

"I sensed that. Look, don't worry too much. We'll get to the bottom of this eventually. In the meantime," he stood up, "I need to get some sleep. You look like you could use some as well."

She followed him out into the corridor. The man in the next room was still calling out for the doctor.

"Inoperable bone cancer," the young doctor grimaced. "We haven't figured out who Doctor Stefanovic is yet. No one by that name works here."

• • •

There it was — the gold Barracuda gleaming under the security lights. But no Gunnar inside. It wasn't until she got up close that she saw him, lying on his back, the driver's seat fully reclined, a forearm flung over his face.

She tapped softly on the window.

He reached over to let her in, eyes hooded in sleep.

He squinted at the light that came on with the door opening.

"How's your mother?"

"Completely out of it."

"What's wrong with her?"

"I'd rather not talk about it now, if that's okay . . . . Can we get out of here?"

"We sure can. Where to now?"

"This is a lot to ask," she said as they neared the parking lot exit, "but do you think you could drive to my mother's place on the coast?"

"No problem."

"Are you sure? You've been driving all day. We could stop at one of the motels on East Burnside," Martha remembering a place called the Riverview.

He shook his head.

"The Sunset Highway can be treacherous after dark."

"Like I said, it's no problem."

They drove through East Portland, a crescent moon shivering in the partly overcast sky, about where Mount Hood usually was.

"You know what the newest thing is in Portland?" he asked as they drove across the Broadway Bridge, the beams of the elevated truss black against the lights of the city. "It's Mexicans. You don't ever see them. There aren't Mexican bars or places they hang out. The only time you hear about them is when they get arrested. Fact is, Mexicans are moving in on organized crime in the Northwest."

"Mexicans," she said numbly.

This was one of those times when life didn't make a lot of sense. Her mother was comatose in a hospital room and here she was talking about Mexican criminals with a man she'd picked up in an elevator, a man who was becoming indispensable to her sanity, though she couldn't put any store on them having a future together.

Beyond the outskirts of the city, they made their ascent into the mountains, the car's headlights bouncing off the markers at the side of the road.

"Walla Walla was hell. You couldn't trust anyone. Compared to Walla Walla, Vietnam was a piece of cake. You know, I got close to some guys over there, including some black guys. I never felt lonely in the army. Not the way I have here."

She read the names on the mailboxes, phosphorescent red letters jumping out at her. The Carlsons, Hansens, Steensons interspersed with Hare, Hunt, Burn, Lark, Wray, compact English names.

"The thing about life is you never know what's going to happen next," he said. "That's what makes life so interesting. Life's an adventure. That's why I'm not sure I could ever settle down. Of course, if I met the right person, that might change. Then you might even see me living in a ranch house with a lawn to cut and junipers to trim."

He fiddled with the radio dial but couldn't pick up a clear signal because of the hydro lines overhead.

Her mind drifted. The summer after grade five, the three of them — she and her urbane, good-looking parents — had driven down the coast, Coos Bay, Eureka, Monterey, Laguna, Encinitas, as far as Tijuana.

They'd stayed in cottages with efficiencies, always with a view of the Pacific. Johnson money had made it possible for them to drive a silver Lincoln Continental, with shark's fins and a square back window, push-button controls at the driver's seat.

Each morning, they'd press on to the next town or explore the redwood parks in the interior. Most afternoons, they'd spend a few hours on the beach. Some evenings her mother would make French toast or hard-boil eggs for deluxe salads. But most often they ate in roadside diners, Swedish pancakes loaded up with syrup, roasted chicken sandwiches with thick fries and gravy, greasy cheeseburgers. No soda was permitted in the car because of the fine leather seats. After dinner Martha used to get the keys to the car from her father. She'd sit in the motel parking lot with the doors locked, often for two or three hours, until it got dark, a ten-year-old girl singing along to the radio, memorizing the lyrics. All those hits from the summer of 1964 — "Leader of the Pack," "Last Kiss," "My Boy Lollipop," and her favorite of all, "It Hurts to Be in Love" by Gene Pitney, the music still alive and clear in her mind, twenty-five years later.

One day, they'd stopped at an amusement park in Santa Cruz, gone on the giant roller coaster and the double Ferris wheel. She could almost smell the air, washed with sun and scented with candy floss. She remembered her father in that cowboy hat, playing games in the arcade, like a teenager. James Spencer was a person who expected to be entertained by life. He'd attracted quite a crowd, heaving a sledgehammer onto a membrane, refusing to give up until he'd sent the rubber ball up to ring the bell. Such a showman, though the woman he'd married always put on the greater show.

Martha wouldn't call her father again, that was for sure. Not after the last time she'd called, on his birthday. After about two minutes on the line, he'd said he had to go, he was barbecuing steaks.

She felt her ears pop. They were coming down from the mountains now, getting nearer the coast, a billboard for a Howard Johnson's in Seaside flashing past. At a dimly lit convenience store on the outskirts of Tillamook, they stopped for food, picking up milk, muffins, granola bars, peanut butter and chocolate.

Her mother's property was tucked into the elbow of a high ridge halfway between Bay City and Garibaldi. The highway along here hugged the edge of a cliff. Where the land dropped away, you could look down and see all of Tillamook Bay and Cape Meares in the distance. She told him where to turn off — the cottage was at the end of a private driveway, snubbed back against the rise of land, hidden from the highway below by manzanita bushes. Where the driveway ended, there was a side yard, several thousand square feet of uncut grass.

They pulled up behind Clara's old Dodge. Martha got out and padded across a carpet of pine needles to the unlocked kitchen door. The cottage was in worse shape than she remembered — the pine floorboards loose and mildewed, the wallpaper smudged and peeling, the fridge, about thirty years old, hummed crankily. Water dripped from the swivel faucet in the sink, the forest-green counter was an impossible jumble of appliances, the cords of the toaster, blender, and radio commingled in a rat's nest.

Right away, they sat down at the kitchen table and ate, slathering the muffins with peanut butter and washing them down with glasses of milk. Gunnar took stock of what was in the cupboards, pushing aside liver-colored pill bottles, cereal boxes, and crumpled-up bags of Dad's oatmeal cookies. He found a box of Aunt Jemima pancake mix on the top shelf — no telling how long it'd been there.

"I could make pancakes in the morning."

"Probably not a good idea," she said. "There's no butter."

"They can be made with vegetable oil."

"I wouldn't," she said. "This kitchen is kind of grotty. The cottage probably hasn't been cleaned in six months. I'm sorry. I hope you don't mind."

"I wasn't expecting the Ritz."

"I'm glad," she said and laughed.

She grabbed the bristle broom from the closet and began sweeping the floor, using the broom handle to dislodge the cobwebs in the corners. Then she dusted the hard surfaces and the lamps with wads of moist paper towel.

Gunnar had turned on the television in the living room. The sound bothered her, but she was in no position to say anything. She found some clean flannel sheets on the unpainted wood shelf in the bathroom, put them on the bed in the guest room.

Wandering into her mother's bedroom, she felt the weight of the past, the smell of mildew from the floorboards, the rosewater air freshener, the burlap of the heavy draperies. Nowhere else in the world smelled remotely like this room. Her mother spent a lot of time in dark rooms. One of the symptoms of her lupus was sensitivity to sunlight. An alarm clock shaped like an owl lay face down on the night table. There was a pile of hardcover books on the oak writing desk. Martha lifted up the book on top, *The Coeur d'Alène Mining War of 1892,* it was from the Tillamook Public Library, three years overdue.

She peered into the closet, fingering the clothes, a tattered terry-cloth robe, a cashmere cardigan, some tweed skirts her mother hadn't worn in years and had to spray every autumn because of the moths. Her mother had long ago given up wearing frilly blouses. The floor of the closet was cluttered with house slippers, calf-high rubber boots, and the spiked golf shoes her mother used for hiking. Cardboard boxes stacked at the back contained Mexican pottery, oddly shaped bowls, none of it particularly nice.

The wind had picked up. Martha felt a shard of fresh air pushing through the cottage. It had been a long day. Tomorrow she'd go back to the hospital, she'd speak to the doctor in charge. Gunnar would drive her. She'd have to deal with him later, work out whatever could exist between them. Her mother was all she could think about now, so much still unresolved between them. She'd never known how she really felt about her, still didn't. It was fortunate in a way that her mother had been so out of it in the hospital, since Martha had no idea what she would've said to her then . . . or . . . *at the end.* What had that nurse meant by those words?

Gunnar was sprawled on the flowered couch that had come from the Laurelhurst house. They'd hardly said a word to each other since arriving at the cottage. But it was as if he'd always been here. She'd probably lose him, just like every other man she'd been with. But he was good for her now.

"I'm going to go to bed now," she said, kissing the top of his head as if it was something she'd been doing for years.

"I look forward to meeting your mother tomorrow," he said. "I bet she's a pretty terrific woman."

"She wasn't terrific as a mother. But that's a long story, I wouldn't know where to start."

She went into the bedroom, closed the door and opened the curtains. The rise of the mountains across the bay was lost in the night. The woods outside were empty of sound except for the wind. She got into bed, letting the little white pills dissolve under her tongue, falling asleep to the nattering of a Los Angeles talk show and late-night ads for workshop gizmos and weight-loss programs.

THE SIXTH FLOOR

A handsome man with curly brown hair got up from behind an oak desk. In his open-necked white shirt and pleated kelp-green cotton trousers, Dr. David Kingston looked more like a tennis player than a doctor, though the sink and examining bed and the bound copies of *Rheumatology* and *The New England Journal of Medicine* dating back to 1970 suggested otherwise.

"You've come from Canada, I understand," he said, plucking a dead blossom from the pot of violets on his desk.

Martha had not expected him to be so young. Probably just forty, with a nice address in the West Hills, a million-dollar summer place on the coast, perhaps a yacht.

"I hear there's still good skiing up there this time of year. A friend of mine goes to a resort called Whistler."

Martha said nothing. This doctor and her mother were not likely to have gotten along. *Only the filthy rich ski.*

"How can I help you?" he asked at length.

"My mother seems to be in a coma or something. She doesn't recognize me, doesn't speak . . . her expression's completely blank."

Dr. Kingston frowned, picked up a file from the stack on his desk, sorted through its contents. A full half-minute elapsed before he spoke. "We're still trying to pin down exactly what's wrong. A doctor these days has to be a bit like Dick Tracy, you know, guilty until proven innocent. We're pretty sure she doesn't have a tumor. It could be an inflammation of the brain, but we'll know that for sure only after we eliminate a few other possibilities. So far the blood tests are inconclusive."

"That's something I wondered about," Martha said. "Do you need to take blood every day?"

"Unfortunately we do. Your mother's on a heavy dose of steroids. Which makes her prone to sepsis, a blood infection. We have to monitor that."

"I talked to Dawne, one of the nurses, she says my mother cries out in her sleep."

"Possibly. The steroids may be making her jittery. It's a common reaction," the doctor said as he leafed through the documents in the file. "And steroids aren't the only medication that could be upsetting her right now . . . . " He closed the file, a practiced look of sympathy registering momentarily on his face. "Your mother's not in a lot of pain. We're making sure of that. Her comfort is the primary consideration in everything we're doing now, but if along the way we can discover a little about her disease, we try to do that too."

Martha could hear what the doctor was saying, his words perfectly audible. But the silence was beginning to happen, empty space opening up around her. *The silence happens when you listen for the fear.* She was attuned to the inside of herself now, her heart pounding, cutting her off from the meaning of his words. She struggled to say what she felt. It was a long time, or so it seemed, before she spoke.

"I hope you're not treating her like a guinea pig," she said, the glory of her voice shattering the silence.

The doctor shrugged off the remark. "We could take her off the steroids, but it would aggravate the inflammation. She's on sixty milligrams of a medication called Solu-Cortif. We could reduce it to twenty, I guess. It might calm her down. I'd like to wait, though, until a vascular expert sees her and I'd like to run some tests on her kidneys, perhaps even do a bone-marrow biopsy."

"You know, Dr. Kingston, this is all getting to be too much. I've been thinking a lot about my mother being in the hospital, she's . . . she's all alone up there . . . I'd like to take her home."

"I can't let you do that."

"Why? What difference will it make?"

"First of all, she's in no condition to travel, and second . . . Look. I won't beat around the bush. It's unlikely she'll ever be able to go home, but it's by no means impossible. I'll know better what we're up against by early next week." He stood up and walked her to the door. "Call me on Wednesday."

•   •   •

Sitting cross-legged on Gunnar's groundsheet in Mount Tabor Park, Martha felt the silence covering over the world, the stillness of each moment, the absence of any thread weaving this early November day into the loose fabric of her life. They'd driven here after leaving the hospital annex where Dr. Kingston had his office, picking up smoked turkey sandwiches from a delicatessen on East Burnside. The park, cut into the hills on the east side, overlooked a reservoir that was part of the city's water filtration plant. There was a smell of wet grass and fermented logs.

Gunnar twisted the top off her cranberry juice and handed it to her.

"You're real good company. You know that?"

"No. But it's nice of you to say so."

She watched him snap the tab on his beer, raise the can to his mouth, take a big swig. He was unlike anyone she'd ever met, and yet it seemed natural that he should be with her at that moment.

She remembered coming here on a warm evening, over twenty years ago now, with a tall boy named Todd, they'd both spat into the reservoir below, then kissed. He'd persuaded her to touch little Todd, his penis. That was probably the summer of 1968, the year before her mother had flown to Montreal, meeting up with a brigade of radicals there, members of the Progressive Workers Party booked on a charter flight to Cuba. It was the sugar harvest, an opportunity to work for socialist reconstruction.

Her mother had just split, giving no warning, leaving no forwarding address, no money for food, no checks to cover the payment of utility bills.

"If the going gets rough," she'd said, "call your father. You do have a father."

She did call her father. But not at first. Not until the going got pretty rough.

Her friends had thought it was so cool to be left alone in the house. But it didn't take long for word to get around. Soon older kids she hardly knew were dropping in at all hours, getting stoned on grass and hash in the living room, stealing things, making a big mess everywhere. She'd had to call her father, who alerted the police. In case of emergencies, she was given the number of an officer from the youth bureau, a born-again Christian.

Martha unwrapped her sandwich, turned up the slices of white bread, sniffed the meat and took a bite, deciding no near-term harm could come from it.

"Look at that." Gunnar pointed to a scaly growth on the side of a nearby alder. "Squawroot."

She looked at it blankly, wondering about its significance, its particular function in the order of life. A squirrel scratched out a warning in the distance. With a finger, she traced the outline of the veins on the back of her hand. The earth under the groun;sheet felt warm. Winter seemed a long way off, but it would catch everyone by surprise as it always did.

"I grew up near here," she said. "I wasn't that happy, but I didn't know it. I wasn't that close to my mother, but I'm sad for some reason. For myself. Not for her. I sort of want her to die. I'm not sure there's a lot left for her here . . . I've never seen anyone die."

She contemplated the inky surface of the reservoir. Years ago, a young male student from Reed College had been discovered floating there.

Martha felt the silence again, wondering what it augured this time, remembering what the doctor in Vancouver had said; her problem wasn't fear or even sadness so much as the anger she turned against herself, that anger probably linked to feelings of abandonment that found their natural expression in her fits of panic, all those times she'd freaked for no reason, been afraid to leave her room. *Who is Martha Spencer?*

"When people die," she said, the red bloom of sumac on the crest of the hill catching her eye, "you're not necessarily free of them."

"That's so."

"I'm not sorry my mother's going to die. Is that wrong?"

"Not if it's how you feel."

"She was so naive. She wanted to save the world. The world sure isn't going to save her," Martha said, thinking to herself, where were the Cuban sugar workers and the Chicano grape pickers now? "She's going to die. I can't stop it. I'm not sure I'd want to stop it now. But I just don't want it happening in that place. I may not love her, but I don't want her dying in there, with strangers shoving her into a body bag while she's still warm."

"No one wants their mother to die in a hospital."

"Remember yesterday, the ranger feeding the elk up in the mountains . . . well, I realized something then, the universe rules itself, human beings are mostly ignorant of that," she said, wondering if she was beginning to speak like him, maybe even think like him. "They won't release her. Not to me they won't. But she deserves better than to die in there. Not because she's my mother, but because she's a helpless defenseless animal. We all are."

"You're right about that. Prison taught me that."

• • •

A television roared demonically in the empty lounge on the sixth floor, drowning out the coughing and moaning of sick people. Visiting hours were over. The lights had been dimmed in the corridor. With no elective surgery scheduled for the weekend, only a handful of nurses were on duty.

"My mother doesn't look well," Martha said to a frowning middle-aged nurse, a small-boned woman with short, dyed red hair. "Could you come and have a look at her?"

The nurse's shoes squished on the floor as they walked from the nursing station to her mother's room.

"Is this gentleman with you?"

Gunnar was in the chair, feet propped up on the windowsill. He raised his hand to his forehead in mock salute.

"What's the problem exactly?" the nurse asked, bending down to listen to her mother's breathing. "Mrs. Spencer is sleeping."

"We want you to unhook her, to remove the IV and the catheter. We're taking her home."

"What! . . . Don't be silly."

"She wants to die at home."

"How would you know what she wants?"

"She's my mother. I know what she wants and I intend to respect her wishes."

"This is a practical joke. You're playing a practical joke, am I right?"

"This is no joke."

"Look, miss, you're upset at seeing your mother like this. It's a natural reaction. What you need, I'm sure, is just a good night's sleep."

The nurse jabbed the call button beside the bed, fear beginning to register in her watery blue eyes.

A voice crackled at the other end of the intercom.

"Code 40," the nurse shouted. "Oscar to Room 647 stat."

Gunnar spoke for the first time. "Don't fuck with us, lady."

"I beg your pardon," the nurse shot back. "How dare you speak to me like that!" She wagged her finger at Gunnar, then turned to Martha, her Adam's apple bobbing as she spoke. "You don't know what you're doing. You really don't."

"Look, lady. Spare us the lecture and do your thing," Gunnar said, jumping up and pulling the door to the room closed. "That means now."

"All right. All right. Let's all of us calm down now," the nurse said as she tucked in the bed covers, using the backs of her hands to lift the thin mattress. "The way you're feeling is quite normal. We see it often on this floor, but it's silly, there are many, many things we can still do for your mother."

"I'm sure there are," Martha said, feeling some of Gunnar's energy flow into her. "But my mother's coming with us. That's all there is to it."

"I can't let you take her."

"Unhook her," Gunnar snarled. "Stop stalling. Just get the fuck on with it."

"I'd like to help you," the nurse retorted. "But I can't. You see I'm not an IV nurse." She pressed the call button again. "Code 40."

"Shut the fuck up. I don't know what you're trying to prove. But if I were you, I wouldn't screw us around with this Code 40 bullshit."

At that moment, the door banged open and a security guard blew into the room, a Filipino in a khaki uniform, a walkie-talkie crackling in his hand.

"What's up?"

"Oscar, we've got a little problem. Mrs. Spencer's daughter here is upset and this gentleman isn't helping matters. Could you please escort them out of the hospital. Visiting hours were officially over at nine."

The guard turned toward Martha, irritation written on his round face. "That's so. I'm sorry, Miss. You must go now."

Martha clung to the edge of the bed.

A triumphant smile spread across the nurse's face. "Explain to them, Oscar, they're trespassing on hospital property."

"Sorry, it's time to go." He pressed close to Gunnar. "Sir, please. Outside."

Gunnar took half a step toward the door, then pivoted and delivered a blow to the security guard's solar plexus. As the guard doubled up, Gunnar came down with a judo chop to the back of his head. "Who the fuck do you think you are?" he shouted. "Barging in here."

The guard collapsed onto the floor.

Gunnar fell on him. They wrestled, arms and legs bumping into the base of the bed.

The Filipino had somehow got a grip on Gunnar's long hair and was tearing at his ear.

"Stop! Stop! This is madness," the nurse shouted, lurching forward, trying to squeeze past Martha to the door.

But Martha was ready. Forearms raised to protect her face and throat, she pushed the nurse back into the corner, absorbing several blows from the nurse's bony hands.

Both women looked on as Gunnar broke away from the guard's grip and landed a hard punch to his mouth.

Then the nurse tried to bolt again, grabbing Martha's arm in an attempt to swing her out of the way, but Martha astonished herself by jerking free, hammering her fist into the nurse's abdomen and shoving her against the wall.

Gunnar had the guard in a headlock. "I don't want to have to mess you up, but I will."

Martha pressed her shoulder against the nurse's chest, keeping her pinned to the wall. Looking down, she saw Gunnar's wrists lock around the security guard's neck, then watched in fascination as he went suddenly lifeless, crumpling into an inert mass on the mottled tile floor.

"Something I learned in 'Nam, a judo choke," he said as he turned over the body. "He'll be out a while."

It was all happening in slow motion. Gunnar was bending down now, taking the revolver out of the guard's open holster, pointing it at the nurse, saying, "Okay. Get on with it."

The nurse cowered at the side of the bed.

"Get the fuck on with it!"

The nurse undid her mother's gown at the back, pulled it away from her shoulders. There was just enough light to work with, no one thinking to click on the overhead lamp. With one deft movement, the nurse tore away the bandage just below her mother's collar bone. Then she removed the dressing and yanked a long needle from the spot, her mother's chest heaving, the reddened flesh puckering around the hole.

The nurse pressed the flesh with a gauze pad that had been part of the original dressing. "If you take her away, she'll be dead in twenty-four hours. You can't just take her off steroids. She has to be weaned."

A voice crackled over the walkie-talkie, telling Oscar to call in. Gunnar picked up the apparatus from the floor and shook it, the voice continued to speak. He took the apparatus to the bathroom and dropped it into the toilet.

"That man's dangerous," the nurse said.

Martha laughed.

"You're killing her. You really are. If you care about your mother, you'll listen to me. If you take her off this medication suddenly, she'll die . . . she'll have a massive heart attack. It won't be pretty." The nurse continued to press on the wound in her mother's chest. "The police will charge you with first-degree murder and I'll testify, you can be sure of that."

Martha opened the drawer in the bedside night table, grabbed a jar of Vaseline, a tin of baby powder, a bottle of Dettol and a pink comb, then threw it all into her mother's handbag.

Her mother's swollen feet wouldn't fit into the brown dress pumps Martha found on the floor of the closet. She grabbed a pair of thick socks from the top shelf, pulled them over her mother's scabbed ankles, thinking there was no time to dress her properly, to get her into the dress she'd worn into the hospital.

Gunnar stripped the bed, wrapped her mother in a sheet and blanket, then ran out into the corridor. The nurses' station was unattended.

Things just accelerated after that. The corridor was a blur of signs. Down the elevator, past the darkened windows of the gift shop, out the swinging glass doors, across the lawn, leaves fluttering down in the wind. Gunnar carried her mother in his arms like a child. Everything was unfolding according to some preordained plan. They were gods.

JEWEL BEACH

It was Saturday night, so there was lots of traffic. Gunnar sped down North Williams, darting from lane to lane.

"If the cops stop us," he said, "we'll say it's an emergency, we'll say we're on our way to the hospital."

Nearing the Broadway Bridge, they had to slow down, a police officer was in the middle of the road ahead, letting a line of cars out of the parking lot at the Coliseum. Martha read the red block letters on the marquée — HOME OF THE TRAIL BLAZERS AND WINTER-HAWKS. The message on the second line was more cryptic, KAM-LOOPS SATURDAY 8 PM. Kamloops was a town somewhere in British Columbia.

Eventually they got free of the traffic jam and crossed the Willamette River.

"We'd better avoid the Sunset Highway," Gunnar said. "I know this other road to the coast. It veers north into Columbia County. We can hook up with it."

Gunnar's road was a two-lane highway with no shoulder. Trees and rock flashed past, little evidence of civilization here except for the occasional cinder-block shack with a tar-paper roof. This was a thinly inhabited part of the state used to tough times. Farther up into the mountains, the sky turned black and it began to rain, pellets of ice bouncing off the windshield. Gunnar slowed down, doing no more than thirty on the slippery winding road. They drove for about four hours, making it as far as Mist, a crossroads hamlet about thirty miles south of Clatskanie. Just beyond the traffic light at the main intersection, Gunnar pulled up in front of the Crazy Horse Motel, a shoebox of a building folded back into a grove of scraggly cedars. They got out, Gunnar making his way over to the office, disappearing behind a beat-up truck with a front-end snowplow, Martha strolling over to look at the life-size plaster horse out front, its smooth dark body whitened by the flurries. She stretched her arms over her head, thinking that if she hadn't followed her feelings, hadn't gone back to the sixth floor of that hospital, she could be safe now, she and Gunnar could be here alone. One day perhaps, they could rent a cottage together, something along the lines of Dun Workin' Manor, the log cabin she'd seen on the drive down from Seattle.

She went back to the car to check on her mother, flicking on the roof light, recoiling at a face made unfamiliar by its distress, the cheeks a latticework of plaques, the mouth twitching and tightening in pain, the eyes drowning in confusion. Whatever was unresolved between them couldn't be settled now. It was no longer a matter of trying to win her mother's love. She'd have to look after things herself as she'd always done.

Gunnar backed up the car in front of the door farthest from the office. Only one other unit seemed occupied. They carried her mother into the chilly motel room, laying her down on top of one of the beds, Gunnar looking for blankets in the closet. The wind wailed outside, rattling the aluminum storms. But the sound wasn't enough to drown out her mother's whimpering.

Martha watched as Gunnar pulled off the torn, urine-soaked hospital gown and lifted her mother's emaciated frame, angling it into the bed between the sheets, then piling on several blankets. She stood there helplessly, wincing each time her mother gagged and cried out. She was unable to look at her mother's haggard face and hollowed-out eyes, her jaw going slack, then tightening every few seconds. It came to her then what she should do. She fetched two fat Percocet tablets from the stash in her bag and cut them with nail scissors on the dusty bathroom counter. Taking the powdery morsels in the palm of her hand, she knelt down beside the bed and slowly fed her mother, getting her to wash down the morsels with little sips of water. Cradling her mother's head in her arms, she tried to hush her up, tried to stop the mewling that issued from her canker-lipped mouth. Even if her mother couldn't fully grasp what was happening, it occurred to her then that she should say something, offer some kind of explanation, but there was nothing she wanted to say, no words came to her.

Resigning herself to the impossibility of breathing warmth into what felt like a corpse, Martha stood up and went to the window, pulling aside the drapery and looking out at the frozen yard, remembering a fight she and her mother had had the year she'd left for the Naropa Institute in Colorado. Her mother had mocked her for being interested in Buddhism, called her a bourgeois flake. She'd retaliated, wounding her mother with the words Portland floozy. It occurred to Martha then that taking her mother out of the hospital was the kind of thing her mother would do. She'd always acted first, thought about the consequences later. And that was what Martha was doing now. She was doing a 'Clara' on Clara. Too bad her mother was too far gone to appreciate the irony.

She could see Gunnar in front of the mirror in the bathroom, his bare shoulder blanched by fluorescent light, his ear red from the scrap with the security guard. Sensing her gaze, he came over and began rubbing her shoulders. His touch was pleasant, but it wasn't what she wanted then. Not with her mother in the room, guilt making it impossible for her to receive the affection this man so freely wanted to bestow. She understood then, clearly and for the first time in her life, that guilt comes when you don't love someone you think you should.

She asked him to sit on the bed, then knelt down on the orange shag carpet and began to massage the muscles and tendons in his long legs. Her thoughts, while she pleasured him, were all over the map. She listened to the inside of herself, knowing that fear could hit at any time, cutting her off from everything. Yet at that moment she felt impregnable, almost serene in his presence. Their meeting seemed fated; they were two outcasts caught up in the sensual magic of what might seem a transgression but was really an affirmation, an assault on finitude.

• • •

She rolled out of the lumpy bed, glimpsing Gunnar in the bathroom, wringing out a towel in the sink. An acrid smell filled the room.

"What's that smell?"

"Some lunchbucket's out back burning garbage. Must not know plastic bottles aren't biodegradable."

There was another smell. From her mother. She'd soiled the bed during the night. Gunnar was using a wet towel to clean her bottom and thighs. Martha watched as he patted her dry.

He'd taken to calling her Miss Clara.

"Your daughter's awake now, Miss Clara," he said. "Say hello to your daughter. Right over there."

Martha choked at the sight of her mother's feet, swollen and scabbed, worse in a way than her arms, bruised purplish yellow from the daily extraction of blood.

Gunnar sprinkled baby powder over the pustulated sores on her mother's buttocks, the cracked skin hanging loose, thick and grayish, like the hide of an elephant.

"I have a lot to thank you for, Miss Clara," he said. "Your daughter is pretty terrific. I guess you must've had something to do with that. Am I right?"

No inkling of understanding appeared in her mother's eyes, only weary confusion. Her whimpering lacerated the stillness of the morning. Martha broke up another Percocet, coaxing the powdery white nuggets down her mother's throat with tiny sips of water. Then they bundled her into the back of the car, propping her head on pillows so she could breathe more easily. They followed a gravel logging road that cut north into the shadow of Saddle Mountain. From the east, light came slanting through the mist into each valley, spearing across the rear window, falling over Clara's clenched jaw.

The sun was not quite up when they got to Necancium Junction and turned south on old Highway 53, her mother beginning to fidget. At least she was out of that hospital, with its blaring intercoms and its late-night visits to the X-ray lab, she was free of all the tubes, the IV fluids rotting her insides, destroying any peace of mind so the last five minutes, the last minute when it came, would be meaningless, a mockery of everything that had gone on before. Taking her mother out of the hospital was no great act of love. It was just the right thing to do, what one human being owed another.

On the coast at Nehalem Bay, Gunnar pulled over at an outlook and flung the security guard's revolver into the thrashing water below, then disappeared into a maze of manzanita. Martha stood by the car, wind blowing the hair up off her forehead. She could see all of Tillamook Bay in the distance. The water, protected from the surf by a long spit of land, was almost still, robin's egg blue. Fishermen had parked their pickups on the south shore road near the boat-launching station. The hardest-working people in the area, her mother used to say, were the fishermen.

They continued down the coastal highway, Martha wishing she was eight years old again, her mother in the front seat, regaling them with tales about a lost gold mine or the treasure buried on Neahkahnie Mountain. Bypassing Tillamook, they drove fifteen miles south in the direction of Jewel Beach. The road twisted down from the high cliffs through meadows of fawn lilies and sweet alyssum. The area was virtually uninhabited, the tides having for millennia pushed the sand farther inland, turning the bay into a latticework of lagoons. She could hear her mother saying Oregon was too beautiful to be a part of the Union, it'd be a free state today if a handful of power-hungry white men hadn't conned the people into joining up around the time of the Civil War.

At a crossroads about a mile from the ocean, they turned down toward the beach, pulling up beside a charred picnic table, half a dozen soda and beer cans strewn over the sand. The marshy land here was glorious, the sun catching the goldenrod and wilting stalks of corn-flower.

Getting out of the car, Martha began to tremble, shrinking from the sight of her mother, who was writhing and jerking now, her breathing rapid and shallow.

Gunnar climbed into the back and gently stroked her face, resting a calming hand on her forehead. "If you feel like taking a walk," he said, "I'll stay with Miss Clara."

Martha took off her shoes and waded into the shallow water, ridges of sand tickling her feet. She made her way toward the end of the spit of land where the bay opened to the ocean, the surf's roar and the shrieking of gulls filling her ears. A memory of a summer day years ago came to her. She'd been pulled out to sea by a sneaker wave, her mother had come after her, dragged her back to the shore, stubbing and bloodying her feet on the rocks. Martha had never again felt as close to her mother as she did that day.

Something red flashed in among the reeds and bushes ahead. Moments later, a dune buggy flared into view, then disappeared, obscured by the dunes and scrub gorse close to the shore. A minute or so later, it reeled up twenty feet away, tilting preposterously to one side before righting itself as it landed on the beach. A woman with long blonde hair waved, her male companion turned the wheel sharply so the vehicle tore off in the direction from which it had come, spinning grains of sand in its wake, breaking the spell cast by Jewel Beach. The dune buggy had no place here. It was like coming across a pelican strangled by the discarded plastic holder of a six-pack.

Retracing her footprints, Martha listened for the dune buggy but heard nothing, the wind from the ocean carrying the noise off toward the north cliffs. An air force jet crossed the sky above the mountains, a glint of silver pushing up into the blue, leaving a thin white trail behind it.

•   •   •

Something was wrong back at the car. Martha reached for her mother's bruised hand.

"She's out of her misery."

"What?"

"She's gone. Your mother's gone."

Her mother wasn't breathing, her hand was cold. Her face was obscenely vacant, her eyes were closed, thank God, but her mouth was shriveled, lifeless, doll-like.

Gunnar showed her how he'd done it. A choke hold, a maneuver from judo.

"It made no sense the way she was suffering."

She looked up at the mountains half-mooned around the bay. A hint of gloom hung in the distance, a foil to the bright pounding sea. Then sadness hit her. She had the rest of her life to live, and now she'd have to live it without her mother.

Gunnar pulled a coarse blanket up over her mother's face.

"Her breathing, fast and shallow like that, meant she only had a few hours anyway."

There was no logic to the situation, nothing really to do or say, and yet it seemed logical at that moment to drive back with the corpse to her mother's cottage.

Rocks, bushes, trees and now and then a clearing with a forlorn cottage in it flew past, Martha sitting in numb disbelief, feeling some compulsion to create meaning here, but finding herself with nothing to measure her mother's life against. She hadn't even made it to seventy. Her fiftieth birthday seemed like it was just a few years ago. Martha remembered hanging crepe streamers in the living room of the house in Laurelhurst. Her mother and her professor friends from Portland State had worn party hats, danced to the Rolling Stones and Jefferson Airplane on the terrace in the garden, then, around midnight, released balloons of hope into the sky. That was 1970, her last year of high school, her mother too high to notice that she was just scraping by, blowing any chance she might've had of getting into college. That same summer, before her mother could split again, she'd been the one who split, following Rob Sinclair, a guy she didn't know that well, to the Haight.

"I'm going to drive into Tillamook," Gunnar said. "I need something to drink."

Very little in the center of Tillamook had changed, the old general store on the main street looked as it had twenty years ago. Gunnar parked out front and Martha went in and bought a six-pack of beer and a carton of apple juice, a loaf of bread and package of smoked ham, and several bags of onion-flavored and salt-and-vinegar potato chips. On the way out, she stopped to read the community billboard — the business cards of roofers and real estate agents and the usual handwritten notes offering to sell washing machines and firewood. There was a request for information about a missing dog named Breeze, an Alaskan husky last seen on the Trask River Road five miles east of town.

Next door, someone had opened an ice-cream parlor and laid down an orange brick patio. Not knowing why, Martha went in. Waiting for the woman to scoop a gallon of banana ice cream into a plastic container, she looked out at the gold car, Gunnar fiddling with the radio dial, mumbling something to himself, then reaching back to grab the empty Nalgene water bottle on the folded-down back seat, seemingly oblivious to . . . to her mother, wrapped in a blanket under a groundsheet in among fishing gear and bags of dirty laundry, apparently dead.

Gunnar had tuned in to a country-and-western station. Though it was only twenty-five miles from town to the cottage, it was Sunday, just past noon, a lot of traffic on the road. Day trippers from Portland. Properties in Tillamook County were in demand. But the locals weren't selling. Happy to sign on with the logging operators in the spring when they were broke, they'd be back after five or six months, usually before Halloween. You'd see them in their junk-strewn front yards, tinkering with their cars before it got dark.

Gunnar parked in the clearing at the side of the cottage, pulling up all the way to the kitchen door so the car was hidden from the driveway. They laid her mother, already stiff with death, on the flow-ered couch. Then they sat down at the kitchen table and ate the banana ice cream.

"They thought I might be allergic to ice cream," Gunnar said. "As a kid, I suffered from hives. They gave me cortisone pills for it. It cleared up as I got older."

A large black fly buzzed in the sun at the screen door.

"That fly knows winter's coming," he said.

There was less light in the kitchen than she remembered. Then she saw why. The manzanita growing up at the front window had to be cut back. It wasn't something her mother would have to worry about now.

"Will you be all right if I leave you alone for a while?"

"I'll be fine."

"I gotta get back to Longview. I'm still on parole, I guess I should have told you that. Anyways every Monday morning, eight o'clock sharp, I have to report to my parole officer and piss in a beaker."

"Don't worry. I'll be fine, really."

"I can stay till it gets dark."

"No. You should go now. I hate long goodbyes."

He got up, a frown clouding his face. They went outside, his boots squishing on the carpet of pine needles.

"Radiator hoses need replacing," he said, Martha looking on, stone-faced, as he checked things under the hood. She hadn't real-ized he was on parole. From the rape nineteen years ago? Or was he in trouble for something else? Or was it that, as her mother had been saying recently, the country was going crazy locking people up?

"I know it's not the right moment," he said when they kissed goodbye. "But I really like you . . . I want to get to know you."

"It takes people a long time to get to know each other," Martha said, thinking of her mother, after all they'd been through together, still a stranger.

"Maybe that's because people don't want to get to know each other," he said. "The thing you should know about me is I'm usually in a hurry."

She didn't know what to say. She knew she needed him and she knew she might never see him again.

"My name's Gunnar Olson, right?"

She nodded.

"Which makes my initials, G. O., right?"

"Right."

"Well, I live by those initials. If there's something I want, I always G.O. go for it."

She knew if she laughed then, he wouldn't understand. She also knew that any laughter, any show of emotion, was dangerous. She withdrew into herself, as she always had. She could hear him speaking, but there was the familiar silence there too. She was in control. *You're never in control.*

"We'll have time to get to know each other when all this blows over. You'll get over losing Miss Clara. It'll take time, but you will. Things will work out, for you, for us, you'll see, world's not ending any time soon."

She watched the gold car disappear around the sumac bushes at the bend in the driveway. For the longest time afterward, she leaned against a birch tree, listening to the long grasses rustling in the breeze, letting the wetness in the air ride up into her nostrils. Then she stood in the middle of the yard, arms crossed, gazing at the cottage. A section of roof was beginning to rot and the clapboard walls, once a teal blue, were now blistered and gray, in need of paint. The screens in the windows had been mended with masking tape. At some point, she'd have to think about what to do, whether to schedule some repairs, in the event there was still money left in the estate.

She went over and got into her mother's old Dodge. The car hadn't been driven in years but the interior still reeked of cigarette smoke. The door to the glove compartment hung down, its clasp broken. The push-button transmission was locked in the P position.

She pressed all the buttons. The car would be worth something, if she could find the keys.

Now was the time for tears, but she knew none would come. *Everything is emotional.* Gunnar was right about that. But sometimes you just couldn't afford to feel things. Loss of one kind or another was what she'd known all her life. In the future, she'd look back on this day, and it would be a day that she'd gotten through, and that was what life was ultimately about — getting through.

Back inside the cottage, Martha wondered if some ritual might help her make sense of the corpse on the couch. She remembered the Hornby Island Buddhists talking about different realms of existence, the need to free the spirit from the body's vessel. If they were here, they'd want to perform some kind of last rites, they'd worry her mother might be reincarnated as another human being, the egotism of our species dooming us to perpetual suffering.

She looked around the cottage, noticing that the luster from the mahogany sideboard, one of the nicer pieces from the Laurelhurst house, was gone. It'd looked fine a few summers ago. Perhaps her mother had scrubbed it with an abrasive cleaner. The glass coffee table was smeared with something sticky, spilled raspberry seltzer probably, and a residue of scum coated the crystal bowl her mother had kept topped up with wrapped toffee squares and squishy jelly beans.

Martha washed her hands in the kitchen sink. Not one smile of recognition at the end. But what did she expect? Her mother had always been too busy to take note of her. As she dried her hands on the dishcloth, she made herself look at the corpse. Through a patch of weak sunlight, she saw that her mother's skin was liverish, her fingers now a charcoal black. It occurred to her then that the powers that be ought to know about this. She looked in the Tillamook phone book for the number of the walk-in clinic, called up and asked the voice at the end of the line if someone could come and take her mother's body away.